A WINTER CREST CHRISTMAS: HONESTY & TRUST

K. RENEE

❀ Created with Vellum

Chapter One

TRUST

I got a call from my homie Saud, and the shit he just told me had me ready to fuck some shit up. I didn't let a lot of people in my circle 'cause it was hard to figure out the real niggas from the fake ones. Me, Saud, and my homie Von have been tight since middle school, and they were the only ones besides my baby brother Taj that I trusted.

When I started out in the game, it was just me and Saud. Once I got shit together, I brought in Taj and Von. My mom busted her ass to take care of us, while she went back to school to get her business degree. Taj and I were only a year apart, and we looked out for one another. It was hard watching the kids in the neighborhood ride their brand-new bikes, rocking the hottest clothes and sneakers while we were getting our shit from Goodwill. Or somebody would hand my mom a bag of clothes that they kids couldn't wear anymore.

Even though we were grateful for it, I wanted new shit for me and my brother, and sometimes she couldn't afford to get it for us. I remember walking home from school one day, and just as I did every day, I went into the corner store to get me two bags of chips, a honey bun, and an Arizona fruit punch. Some dude came in the store looking like he was in a hurry, but he walked up to me and told me to put this bag in my backpack. He said he would pay me two hundred dollars if I did that favor for him, and he wanted me to meet him back here tonight at nine. All I could think about was that two hundred dollars and the shit I could buy for me and Taj. So, I quickly pulled my damn books out and stuffed his bag in my book bag. Walking to the counter, I paid for my things.

"Don't you get mixed up in nothing with these dudes out here, Trust. Regina is doing the best she can for you boys. It would kill her if something happened to you and your brother," Mr. Ted said to me, handing me my bag.

"I'm not." Is all I said, and I walked out of the store. By the time I made it to the corner of my block, people were all standing around, and all I could hear was that they killed him in broad daylight. When I got closer, it was the dude that gave me the bag in the store. I was standing there in shock. I looked around to make sure no one was watching me, I wondered what or who the hell he was running from or what he had gotten me into. I ran home and went straight to my room; Taj was at the park hanging out with his friends and my mom was at work. Pulling the bag from my book bag, I dumped it out on my bed, and my eyes got big as shit. There was weed, cocaine, and six stacks of money wrapped up. Each stack had nothing but hundred-dollar bills. I couldn't believe what I was seeing. This shit was about to change our lives forever. But I had to play it cool and be smart about my next move.

For a couple of months, I sat on it and did nothing. I came up with a plan, did my research, and waited to see if anyone would approach me about dude. I started making small moves, putting my plan into motion, selling the weed in school, and cocaine and weed in the neighborhood. Because my mom worked and went to school, that gave me the space to move how I wanted to in the streets. She wasn't able to watch us the way she wanted to, and that's how the streets got us.

The only father figure I had was Taj's pop. Even though him and our mom wasn't together, whatever he did for Taj, he did for me. I had nothing but respect for that man, and that's why I take care of him the way that I do. He's gonna forever be my Pop. I didn't know who my real dad was, and every time I asked my mom, she said he didn't want anything to do with us. After a while, I stopped asking her, and he was never mentioned in our house again. I grew up hating that nigga, but also wanting to know what was wrong with me and why he didn't want me.

I've been in the game since I was fifteen, and I had no plans on leaving anytime soon. Hell, I was just getting started. I was a rich nigga for sure, but I wanted to be wealthy. There is definitely a difference in that shit. I've always wondered would my life be different if my real dad was in the picture. I'm twenty-six years old now, so wondering about that nigga and how my life would be is irrelevant, I guess. Pulling up next to Saud's truck, I rolled down the window, and Taj was sitting in the car with him.

"Are y'all sure she's in there?" I questioned.

"Bro, I was out having dinner with Shantay at Relish, and I saw her and that nigga having dinner. I eased the hell out of there, called Shantay an Uber, waited for them to leave the restaurant, and followed them here. They've been in the house for about an hour now." He dropped his head, still in disbelief at what had transpired.

"I just pulled up about ten minutes ago. All I know is this shit is fucked up!" Taj stated. If it was true, it was more than fucked up. I quickly pulled my car over, got out, and headed up the street to the house. It was Christmas Eve, and this the shit she was out here doing. The crazy part about all of this shit was I had just proposed to this bitch last month on her birthday. And to find out that she's inside the house with my best friend! Yeah, I'm about to kill these muthafuckas! Pulling my gun from my waist and sliding my key inside the lock, I unlocked the door. We all had keys to each other's cribs, just in case of an emergency. Walking into the house, their clothes were strewn across the floor and staircase.

"Damn, bro. I was praying that this nigga wasn't on no flaw shit. If that nigga up there fuckin' Brielle, I'm with whatever you with." Taj already knew what it was with me.

"Same with me, it's whatever with me." Saud shrugged. This nigga Von supposed to be my homie, and he on some bullshit. I don't play that disrespect shit! I would've never fucked on his bitch or did no shit like this to him. Moving upstairs, we could hear the music, and the moans from them fucking. I eased the door open, and the moment I saw my best friend fucking her from behind is the moment I lost my damn mind.

"Nigga, this the type of fuck shit you on!" I yelled, and they both jumped away from each other.

"Trust, oh shit!" Brielle screamed out, trying to cover herself with the sheets on the bed.

"Nahhh, nigga! Kill these muthafuckas! He was tearing her ass out the woodwork. A nigga can't live to talk about how he was digging in my used-to-be bitch before she became my dead bitch!" Taj spoke, shaking his head.

"Fuck, bro! I know it looks fucked up, and I know she's your girl! But this bitch ain't loyal! She been throwing the pussy at me. I got fucked up and I slipped up with her. You been my boy since we were lil' niggas. And I know you not gone kill me over some hoe ass bitch. She doesn't mean shit to me. I just slipped, bro. It was a mistake that shouldn't have happened. It's always bros before hoes, right?!" This nigga was fucked up and slow as fuck.

"Nigga, a slip-up?! A mistake! You obviously wanted to fuck, so that's what the fuck you did! Stand on that shit You a flaw ass nigga for this shit, and I'll never fuck with yo' bitch ass again." I was ready to blow this nigga head off.

"Again! Nigga! I'll never give that nigga the again option, the fuck!" Taj blurted.

"Taj, fuck you! You think you better than us, because this nigga yo' brother! You always been a cocky nigga. I can't wait for the day a nigga put one in your pussy ass dome," Von gritted a Taj.

"Bruh, I'm not my fuckin' brother! I'll murk yo' ass in front of your mama and kill her ass for making a flaw ass nigga like you. Pussy muthafucka!" Taj gritted with his gun on Von, itching to pull the trigger.

"Taj! I got this, bro," I told him.

"Nigga, I'm your best friend, and you acting like this over this bitch! Fuck it, it's gone be what it's gone be! Let me let y'all in on a lil' secret. She never loved you, homie! She was just with you stacking her bread and setting your dumb ass up for me. That's who Brielle is. She

4

ain't never gone be loyal to a nigga like you. She was with you because I put her with you, nigga! That's my bitch! You weren't supposed to find out about this shit, because she was gonna kill yo' ass tonight while you slept. I just wanted to dig in the pussy first. I should've let her handle her business and knock yo' bitch ass off first!" This nigga smirked.

"Yo, what the fuck is this nigga talking about?" Saud questioned, pulling his gun out.

"Nigga, fuck you! Me and you were homies before these niggas, but you out here riding Trust's dick like some down ass bitch! Look at you, yo' bitch ass ready to kill me over this nigga?! That's the problem! Everybody always ready to jump when this nigga say jump and go to war when he says let's go to war! I'm tired of that shit! I'm tired of hoes always jumping on his dick! I'm tired of this nigga spending money without a care in the world and I'm out here watching every penny I spend! I want it all and I'ma get that shit!" He roared with spittle flying all over the place.

"Wheeewww! Shoot this nigga before I do!" Taj looked over at me.

"Normally, you would've been dead before you could climb out of the pussy. I wanted to hear what your flaw ass had to say before I let off on your ass."

"Trust! You can't believe him. I would never do anything to hurt you, baby!" Bri cried.

"Bitch, you were gone climb off my dick, go home, and blow this nigga brains out on Christmas morning. Merry Christmas, nigga!" Von looked over at me and then at Brielle with his face twisted. Before he could form his next sentence, I sent two shots to his head, and Brielle started screaming and crying out for her nigga.

"Please! Don't kill me, please! I'm so sorry! Please forgive me, baby! Please, I love you so much! This was a big mistake! It never should've happened; I swear he didn't mean anything to me!" She cried hysterically, trying to approach me.

"Bitch! Suck my dick!" I growled, sending two shots to her muthafuckin' head. To know that this bitch was on some grimy, flaw ass shit had me on one. I wanted to unload this clip in her ass, and that's exactly what the fuck I did.

"Urgggghhhhhhh! Fuck!" I roared.

"How could I not know these muthafuckas was out to get at me?!" I turned to look at Taj and Saud.

"Bruh, ion think none of us caught on to his bullshit. I've never seen Brielle before until you started fucking with her, and that's some crazy shit. Because we've always known who each other was fuckin' with. I guess the nigga been on this grimy shit for a while. 'Cause he put a plan together, and had I not seen them out tonight, they would've executed that shit." Saud was right. Shit could've gone left because I would have never seen that shit coming.

That's some fucked up shit to find out from a nigga that was supposed to be yo' bro, and a bitch that was supposed to be the love of your life. Damn, man! I'm sorry you gotta go through this shit. Go ahead and go get your mind right. Me and Saud will clean this shit up," Taj said to me, and I turned and walked out of the room. This shit had my head spinning, and I had to sit in my car and calm down before I drove off.

I've been with Brielle for three years and really loved that girl. She approached me at a block party in the hood, and we hit it off. It took me a minute to commit, but I opened up to it all once I did. It was all love, and I was ready to give this girl the world. And the whole time, she was a bird ass, flaw ass bitch out here trying to set a nigga up! I'll never move the same again. My well-being and my family's well-being is all that matters to me. If you're not a part of my circle now, you'll never be a part of it.

Chapter Two

TRUST

Two Years Later

I was sitting here in my warehouse out in the county, listening to this nigga Case tell me how he accidentally gambled my fuckin' money and lost the shit.

"Trust, I swear, man. I'm gonna get your money! I was trying win my uncle Mike's watch back, and I knew I had the money in the car, so I used it to get back in the game. I've never lost that much money before, and I always get what I lose back. Just give me a lil' time, and I'ma get it all back, I promise!" He pleaded.

"Nigga, do it look like I give a fuck about anything other than you getting my fuckin' money!" I gritted.

"It's always that one muthafucka in every niggas camp that'll die because he done fucked up the plug's money." Taj laughed, as he sat on the table popping some damn M&M's in his mouth.

"The only reason I keep giving you these muthafuckin' passes is because of Mike, nigga! And the fucked-up part is, you know that shit! But one of these days you gone keep playing with me and I'ma send you to lay beside him. You got one fuckin' week to come up with my money. One fuckin' week, nigga! And you better bring that shit to me, don't make me come to your ass 'cause that shit ain't gone go well for you." I headed for the door because I was tired of looking at that nigga.

"You know you gone have to end up killing that lil' nigga, right? He got too much shit going on in these streets, and I can bet he uses our name to get him out of a lot of shit. I know your reasoning for keeping him around, but he's going to cause some bullshit that we don't need to be in. Right now, it's a bag, but later it could be much more than just fifty racks. I heard the nigga out here in some real gambling bullshit," Taj said once he was in the car.

"Let's keep an eye on him, and if it comes to that, it'll be done," I told him and jumped on the highway to head to our mother's house.

* * *

One Week Later

"*D*o we have the new address on that nigga yet?" I questioned, looking over at Taj, and Saud. It just hit me that today was that nigga's deadline to pay me my money. I still can't believe he lost my shit in a dice game. Not to mention, he's out here gambling Mike's shit away instead of cherishing the shit his uncle left behind for him. I've been hearing for a while that the nigga had a gambling problem. I didn't really give a fuck about his personal business; that shit had nothing to do with me until now. The only reason I didn't kill his bitch ass is because his uncle Mike started out in the game with us ten years ago. Mike made sure no one fucked with us, and I was indebted to him for that shit.

He was a solid dude, and when he came to me about helping his nephew, it was no questions asked because that's how much respect I had for him. Mike got killed about a year ago over some chick he was fucking with. We wasted no time finding the nigga that killed him, but the fucked-up part about that shit is, when it was time to strap up and get at them niggas, his damn nephew was nowhere to be found.

To be honest, I still don't think I'm fully recovered from that blow of losing Mike. If you ask me, that nigga Case been a disappointment from the start, and it's fucked up because his uncle loved his funky, dysfunctional ass. Mike is definitely the only reason that pussy nigga still breathing. It's not like I needed that bag, but it's the principle behind that shit.

"Jason sent the address over to me about an hour ago." I was on my feet the moment Saud said we had the new address on Case.

"Ahh hell, this nigga 'bout to be on some bullshit." I heard Taj yell out behind me, and he was right. It was definitely about to be some bullshit. I gave that nigga a deadline to have my shit; he ignored what the fuck I said, and that shit was a slap in my muthafuckin' face. I guess he figured since he moved, we wouldn't be able to find him. I'm not sure who the fuck he thought I was, but I'm never gone be a nigga to play with.

Thirty minutes later, Saud was pulling up on the corner of his block out in South Philly. We got out of the car, and Saud immediately went to work to open the door. We didn't hear an alarm beep, and that shit was crazy to me. The first thing you're supposed to do is protect your temple. The moment we walked into the house, his bitch ass jumped from the couch, trying to go for his gun until he realized it was us.

"Yooo, what the fuck y'all doing?!" He questioned, looking at us like he was appalled that we were in his shit. I'm fuckin' appalled that this nigga playing with my muthafuckin' bread!

"Where the fuck is my money, nigga!" I gritted, gripping his ass up.

"Fuck! Trust, I just need a few more days I can't pull fifty racks outta my ass, my nigga. But you foul as fuck for coming up in my shit like this." He shook his head obviously pissed.

"Funny you say that 'cause yo' bitch ass was able to pull it outta yo' ass when it was time to gamble my shit away! I gave you one week to come up with my bread, and you still don't have my shit!" I gritted, pulling my gun out, and placing that shit to his head. I was mad as fuck that this nigga was playing with me right now.

"Shhhhh, fuck... Don't do this shit, Trust. Let's talk outside. My girl upstairs sleep, and I damn sure don't wanna wake her ass up. I got twenty racks now, and I'll have the rest in two days. Please just give me two days, Trust!" He begged, and I thought about what he just said. Pulling my gun from his head and turning his ass loose, I headed for the stairs.

"Yo, where the fuck are you going?" He questioned, running behind me, but he knew better then to touch me.

"Here we the fuck go!" Taj blurted, pulling his gun from his side. I made it upstairs, and most of the doors were opened, so I instantly moved towards the bedroom that had the closed door. Entering the bedroom, his girl was sound asleep, with a damn mask over her eyes.

"The fuck she got it looking like a winter wonderland in this muthafucka. Look like damn Santa's workshop fell outta the North Pole and landed dead slap in the hood! Da fuck y'all got going on in here? I heard of being Christmassy, but this shit over the top. Damn, is that rain pouring down like that? It's thunder and lightning hard as hell out there. It wasn't a drop of rain when we came in here! I guess that's God crying out to this gun tottin' ass nigga right here for the dumb shit he about to do!" Taj crazy ass looked over at me.

"Nah, that's my girl's sound bar. She likes going to sleep with calming sounds, and she loves when it rains. Come on, man. Please leave her out of this. I'ma get you your money, I swear," Case pleaded, but my mind was made up. Baby girl was coming with me until he got me my bread. I hated to wake Sleeping Beauty up, but she was about to wake up to a big surprise. She could blame her nigga for getting her into this shit. I'm doing everything in my power not to kill this nigga, because I knew how much Mike loved his nothing ass. Lifting shorty from the bed, she nestled her body comfortably into my arms with her head on my chest.

"Hell to the nawl! This nigga 'bout to get us a kidnapping charge. Nigga, you really 'bout to take this nigga bitch in front of him like that?! And nigga, you really gone just let this nigga walk up in yo' shit and take yo' bitch like that? You a pussy, straight up! 'Cause owing a nigga money or not, ain't no nigga walking up in my shit thinking he gone walk out with my bitch. I'm definitely going in Scarface mode and introducing this nigga to all my lil' and big muthafuckin' friends.

Nigga, you ain't got no guns taped under the tables, under the pillowcase, in the refrigerator behind the muthafuckin' eggs, in the Frosted Flakes box in the pantry or nothing? Damn! If I was lil' baby, I would fight for my life with this goon lookin' ass nigga and come out singing Fuck nigga Free out this bitch! I mean, if we outcha on some kidnapping shit now, I guess that's what we doing, but ion gotta like the shit! You my brother, and I'ma stick beside yo' dumb kidnapping ass." Taj shrugged, and I shook my head at his ass.

"Trust, what the fuck, man! Put my girl back in the bed. Honesty, wake yo' dumb ass up! That nigga ain't me!" Case yelled. That's when baby girl pulled her mask off, and her eyes were instantly on me.

"What the fuck is going on!" She yelled, trying to jump out of my arms, but I held on tight, moving down the stairs. Saud moved ahead of me to get the door, just as baby girl started swinging on me and screaming for help. I stopped dead in my tracks to look at her.

"Shorty, it's in your best interest to chill the fuck out. It doesn't matter how much you scream or fight, you're still coming with me! If your nigga get my money like he said he would, then you'll be home in a couple of days!" I gritted, and she calmed her little ass down.

"Case, do something! You can't just let them take me like this!" She cried, and I almost felt bad for involving her in this shit. I just hope this teaches her a lesson about fucking with fuck niggas.

"Fuck! Trust, I'll get your money! Please don't do this shit! Let her go!" Case screamed, trying to run up on me, but he stopped in his tracks when Taj pulled his gun on him.

"Nah, nigga! It's too damn late for all that tough shit now. You should've been giving that boss nigga energy when we came up in yo' shit," he told him.

"Get my money; you get your bitch!" I stated, and kept it moving to the truck.

"Who are you, and what the hell do you want with me? Please don't do this to me!" She cried, trying to open the door, but Saud locked it and pulled off the block, hitting the highway.

"Look, I know this may seem fucked up, but you're just collateral until that nigga brings me what he owes me. You're just collateral until he pays me my bread," I told her, and she started screaming at the top of her lungs.

"Mmmm, mmmm, hit her ass upside the head or summin' 'cause I can't do too much of that shit right there. Ain't that what them niggas do in the movies when they kidnap somebody? I'm good at drug dealing, killing niggas, countin' money, bustin' my guns, bustin' nuts when I'm knee deep in some pussy, and beating a nigga ass. This kidnapping shit ain't for me. Ion got time to be chasing they ass when they're trying to run away. I mean, I might take off behind them for about a minute, and after that, they gone definitely get away. 'Cause who the fuck got time to be chasing niggas in these white people neighborhoods. That's the quickest way to get us a quick five to ten or ten to twenty!

I heard them judges be giving you the time that it be on them clocks when you standing there. Be just our luck that bitch say twenty-five to life! Fuck that! I like my freedom; I don't even want that type of negative narrative in my mindset or talked around me. Jail, judges, and prosecutors are three niggas ion fuck with at all! I need a blunt and a drink!" Taj sounded stressed the fuck out, and I wanted to laugh but now was not the time.

"Christmas is three weeks away!!! It's my favorite time of the year, how could you do something like this?! I have so much planned with my friends, and my cousin is coming to visit me. Please, I don't have shit to do with what Case owes you." She looked over at me, and when she realized I wasn't moved by what she was saying, she started screaming again!

"Girl, shut yo' ass up wit' all that damn hollin'! The nigga don't give a fuck about Christmas, yo friends, or your damn family. His ass taught Scrooge on how to be muthafuckin' Scrooge. You got a betta chance at talking to God and seeing if he can help get yo' ass outta this predicament. Never mind. Just sit back and be quiet, 'cause this nigga might have God on the payroll." Taj shook his head, and Saud was in a fit of laughter. My brother was always so damn animated about everything. I've always been the more serious one out of the two of us.

Lil mama must have taken in what he said because she was no longer screaming, but the tears, and sniffles were in full effect. I've never done anything like this in my life, but I wanted this nigga to know I wasn't playing with him. I'm not sure what my next move with baby girl would be, but I would never hurt her.

We pulled up to my gate, and Saud put in the code. One thing I don't play about is my safety when I'm in my own home. I have security that monitors my house, and the code on my gate changes after every use. A new pin is sent to me, Taj, and Saud every time it's changed.

"I just want you to know that this security system you got is ass. These damn pin numbers is taking up too much space in my phone," Taj complained, as he always does when he comes over to visit. My mom and Grandma just wait until I'm home to come over. The moment Saud stopped the truck, lil mama had a lot to say.

"I'm not getting out of this fucking truck! If you're going to kill me, just do it now. I'm not going in that house for you to torture and rape me all because my stupid ass fiancé owes you some money. Why are you holding me over some dumb shit he did?! I live my life right; I don't get involved in his mess! I just got a new job, and I go to work every day, I go to church whenever I get a chance, and I pray when I wake up in the morning and before I go to bed at night!" She cried, wiping the tears from her eyes.

"Uhhh, ion think God heard them prayers at all today, sis, 'cause you here with this kidnapping ass nigga. Now y'all get out and go handle the business that kidnappers and kidnapees do under these circumstances," Taj ass stated, and I swear I was ready to close line this nigga. I got out of the truck and walked around to get her out of the car. She immediately started screaming, throwing blows, and kicking me.

"Nigga, you should've studied this shit before you decided to go into this kidnapping business 'cause you look uncomfortable as fuck! But take her screaming ass on the outside of the truck! In public, I'ma stick beside you, but now that we here, you on your own!" Taj spoke, and Saud burst out laughing. These two niggas together made my whole ass itch.

As soon as I pulled her hysterical ass out of the truck, these niggas put the car in reverse and sped the fuck off like they were in a high-speed chase. I know this wasn't the smartest thing to do, but it was either this or kill her bitch ass nigga. I shook my head because this girl looked a mess out here. Tear-stained face, red eyes, hair standing all over her head, bare feet, and she had on a mid-thigh silk nightgown. I had to get her inside and situated, so that I could figure out what the fuck to do next.

Chapter Three

HONESTY

I can't believe this shit! I can't believe that I let Case get me into some more bullshit behind him. We've been together for four years, and I'm not gone lie; at one point, the nigga had me gone over his ass. The first couple of years we were together was everything, but the last two, this nigga showed his true colors. I was fighting bitches left and right over his hoe ass and threatening to leave him every damn time. Yet my dumb ass was still with him, and still letting him get me into bullshit after bullshit. Now look at the bullshit I'm in behind his ass. I swear if God gets me out of this situation, I'm leaving that nigga and never looking back.

Dude gripped my arm, pulling me inside of the house, and that shit set me off. I swung on his ass, punching him in his face. I was pissed that he was doing this to me, and at this point, I didn't give a damn about shit. One thing I could do is throw these hands, and that's what it was about to be in this fucking house. If his ass is gonna kill me, I'm not going down without a fight. He grabbed my hands and pinned me up against the door.

"If you put your fuckin' hands on me again, I promise you I'ma fuck yo' little ass up. I told you that I wouldn't hurt you but keep fuckin' with me, and I might change my damn mind!" He gritted in my

15

face. He was so damn close to me, the heat from his breath tickled my damn nose. My gaze moved around his home, admiring the marble floors, cathedral ceilings, chandeliers, and paintings on the walls. The décor was a neutral tan color throughout, with splashes of gold, and burnt orange colors to highlight the rooms. From what I could see so far, this house was definitely touched by a woman or a designer, and they were spot on in making it breathtakingly beautiful.

"Let's go," he angrily spat, pulling me upstairs to one of the bedrooms. When he opened the door, my mouth dropped. This room was just as beautiful as the lower level of the house. It looked as if it was something out of a magazine. There was a king size bed, and a sitting area with a huge television and surround sound. It even had a fully stocked bar in the room, a full bathroom, and a balcony.

Looking over at the owner, I had to stop myself from salivating. His gaze had me captivated, and it was the first time I paid any attention to this man. His eyes were unusually beautiful. They were grey but seemed like specs of blue appeared at times. His skin tone was the color of honey and chocolate mixed; he definitely had a unique complexion and is an extraordinary piece of artwork, that's for sure. I'm not sure where he got it from, but he was beautifully made with his Scrooge ass attitude. This dude was fine as fuck, but I had to remember that the nigga kidnapped me, and my life is in danger.

"Sup, boss. I got your text; I'll have everything done shortly." Some nerdy looking dude appeared in the door. He started working on the locks, pulled out some type of pad, and placed it on the wall.

"He's changing the locks on the door so that I can keep them locked. You will remain in this room when I'm not home. When I'm home, I will allow you to be downstairs with me. You're free to go out on the balcony, just so you know the drop from the balcony is long, and my property is guarded by three security guards twenty-four hours a day. I don't have neighbors close enough to hear you scream, so there is no need to try that. I'm not into hurting women, but I had to prove a point to your nigga. Just know that your stay here will be pleasant, unless you make that shit hard. If that nigga pays me my money, you will be home in plenty enough time to enjoy the holidays with your family." This nigga had the nerve to smile at me.

"Nigga, fuck you with a dirty dick! You could have kept this shit between you and Case! You're not into hurting women, but yet you hurt me when you took me from my home. I just started a new job, and now I'm going to lose it because of you! Stay the fuck away from me because I'm telling you now, I can fight, and I'ma fuck you up every time you come near me!" I spat, and he chuckled.

"If that's how you wanna play it, shorty. You set the tone, and I'll be damn sure to adjust to that shit! Make yourself at home, drink as much as you want, and if you get hungry, just go to the intercom system and hit master, and I can hear you talk. Just let me know what you need, and I'll be sure you get it." He turned to talk to the guy, and about thirty minutes later, they both left the room, locking me inside.

I was scared as shit, but for some reason, I believed him when he said that he wouldn't hurt me. I looked at the clock on the nightstand, and it was going on three in the morning. I just realized that I didn't have anything—no clothes, no phone, nothing. I guess when you're kidnapped, that's how shit goes. I pray Case does the right thing and gets me out of here.

Chapter Four

TAJ

"*M*adear, why yo' ass always hogging the blunt? I'ma stop smoking with yo' ass because you don't know how to smoke fair. Take a few tokes on the shit, and then pass it back."

"You're a drug smuggler, if we run out you can just go to the car and get us some more. You know I told my girlfriend Geraldine from bingo that my grandsons are drug smugglers, and if she ever needed some of that backdoor, I could get her some for the low." She looked over at me as she pulled on the blunt like what she was saying was right.

"Yooo, what the fuck is a backdoor? It's backwood, and that's the type of cigar you roll up with! You need to learn your drug terminology before you start talking that shit like you right. And why the fuck are you telling her some shit like that shit? Madear, you could get us put under the jail. What if Geraldine old ass got family that work for them folks? Then what! She gone have all our asses hemmed up, and all I know is your old ass coming with us." I shook my head, not believing that she was out here calling us smugglers.

My grandma was certified crazy, but she was the homie, and I loved her crazy ass. I hung with Madear more than I hung out in the streets. One thing we were gone always do is talk shit, gossip, eat good, and smoke some good ass weed.

"Nigga, if she gets them people on us, then you gone do what you do best, and take her ass out." She looked at me with her face all twisted.

"Okkkk, don't play wit', Loretta!" I teased her.

"It's Big Lo, not the lil' one!" She snapped her neck in my direction, and we both fell out laughing.

"And that's on Jesus and his disciples!" I blurted, and we fell out laughing even harder. I swear the shit me and Madear be coming up with always had us in a fit of laughter.

"I wonder where your knucklehead ass brother at; I called him twice this morning," she said to me.

"He probably over there trying to figure out how to keep his hostage locked up." I shrugged as I popped a piece of fish in my mouth.

"Hostage! Boy, what the hell you talkin' about?" She questioned, pulling her chair closer to mine.

"All I know is some nigga in the crew owe him some money, and Trust went up in that man shit and took his girl for collateral. He told the nigga to get his money, and he could have his bitch back!" I told her.

"I know you fuckin' lyin'! Ohhh, he went up in there on some El Chapo type shit, huh? That nigga 'bout to do football numbers fuckin' with them drugs and kidnapping charges! He done did his big one with this shit right here. I ain't never seen no kidnapping before, though. Let's go over there and see if he's doing it right before y'all go to jail." She patted me on the back and grabbed her purse.

"I'm not going no damn where, and if yo' ass ain't never seen a kidnapping before, how you gone know if he doing the shit right or not?" I asked her.

"I've seen the shit on television, and I know they know what they're talking about. Now come on, let's go!" Once Madear wanted to do something, she wasn't gonna stop until we did that shit. I got up and headed out the house. I know Trust gone fuck me up for telling Madear. I kept Madear up on all the tea, and the shit he got going on over there was piping hot ass tea. Thirty minutes later, we were pulling into his driveway, and Madear wasted no time getting out the car.

"Trust!" I called out, walking into the house.

"It doesn't look like kidnapping central around here. You know victims sometimes get away from their kidnapper. Lawd, you think she done whooped his ass and got loose?" Madear whispered as we looked around, standing in the foyer of the house.

"What y'all doing here?" Trust questioned from behind, and both me and Madear jumped.

"Wheewww, baby! This shit got us too damn jumpy! Nigga, I heard you got a hostage in here. I wanted to come see you, and tell you how much I love you before them folk come pick you up," she told him, and I burst out laughing because she was serious as hell.

"Can you please help me?! He kidnapped me, and I'm here against my will. Please help me!" Her voice came over the intercom.

"Ahhh, hell to the nawl! Nigga, you gone be on Nancy Grace by your damn self! Chile, she out here begging for help like a real victim. That's what I get for being high and trying to be nosey. Lawd, I don't wanna be an accessorize to the crime. And if you get me outta this situation, lawd, I promise I'ma mind my business. I told my daughter she should've done a better job at raising them, but noooo, she raised some illegal drug smuggling, kidnapping, gun-totin' goons. They some real shooters, and I'ma always ride for them, just not on no ricardo charge (Rico charge)!" She was shaking her head back and forth, and that shit had me on the flo.

"Bruh, you should have thought this through. Ion think kidnappers bring their victims to they real house, and it sounds like you got her upstairs because how is she operating the intercom system? I think yo' ass supposed to throw her in the basement. The fuck am I saying your damn basement is the dopest part of the house. What if we were mama? You know ole girl would've been free by now. You betta keep Regina from over here. That means you gone have to pay Madear to be quiet." I winked at Madear, and she went right into action.

"Yep, I say a cool twenty thou works." She smiled, rocking back and forth.

"Really, Madear!" Trust snapped his neck in her direction.

"Yes, nigga! Really! I got shit to do, now hurry up!" As soon as he walked away, we bust out laughing.

"Madear, why you asked for that much money? You know your old ass wrong for that, trying to shake yo' grandson down like that. You buying us something to eat from Harold's when we leave here. I'm ordering everything I want too!

"So, no one is going to help me! Fuck all of you bitches! Jingle bells, jingle bells jingle all the fuckin' wayyyyyyy! Silenttt night... holy fuckin' nighttt... all is calm, all is muthafuckin' brighttttt! Round yon hoe ass virgin, mother and childddd! I wish I could sleep in heavenly peace..." The crazy chick started singing Christmas songs, and changing up the damn lyrics.

"Ion think you should sing that last part. Cause yo' kidnapper got a lot pieces that will straight send you to sleep in heavenly peace," I spoke into the intercom.

"He damn sure do. She a slow ass victim! Who the fuck sings Christmas carols at a time like this? I'd be out here singing *Man Down by Rihanna*. Let that nigga know it's about to be a muthafuckin' problem. She coulda been up there trying to build her a damn weapon, but noooo, she up there worried about Santa Claus and his funky ass reindeers," Madear said, and I was through with her ass.

"They not even coming to this nigga house 'cause the way that nigga hate Christmas. He gone open fire on they ass before they can land on the roof." I laughed.

"Shut your ass up and get out!" Trust spat, slapping me upside the head with the stack of money.

"Nigga, make that the last time you touch me. Punk ass, amateur ass kidnapper! That's why I hope she get away and beat yo' ass! Lil mama, bite his ankle and run 'cause that nigga crazy!" I said into the intercom, and me and Madear fell out laughing.

"Thank you for the money, Grandson. Call me if you need... You know what, call your mama if you need anything." She kissed his cheek, and we left out. One thing me and Madear gone do is have some damn fun, but her ass just came up on twenty racks, and we were on our way to Harold's Seafood.

* * *

"*A*hhh shit! Harder, Taj!" Zena screamed as I pounded her insides. This girl had some good ass pussy, and that shit always had me over here knee deep in the pussy.

"Fuck!" I growled, gripping her ass as I slammed inside of her. I was hitting that shit so hard, lil mama was damn near hanging off of the bed. A few minutes later, we were both cumming. We lay there for a few minutes trying to catch our breath, and I looked over at the clock. It was a little after eleven, and I still had a stop to make before I headed home.

"I gotta go; I some shit to handle." I smacked Zena on the ass and crawled out of the bed.

"Why do you do that shit? Every time you come over here, it's always I gotta go do this or I gotta go do that. Why don't you ever stay the night?" She pouted, crawling out of the bed to follow me into the bathroom. She could follow me all she wants; she knew the deal with me. I don't stay the night with nobody. I like the peace of sleeping in my bed by myself. I'm not afraid of commitment. If that situation ever arises for me, then I'll be ready, but for now, I'ma continue to do me. Zena isn't my girl. She knows that, she's just someone I'm fucking, and she's not the only chick I'm seeing.

"Zena, how many times do we have to go through this shit? You're not my girl, so why would I stay the night with you? I never gave you the impression that shit was more than what it is. I've always been a buck with you," I told her. I've never been one of those dudes to lie about my intentions. I'll never put a woman through that. I saw what that shit did to my mom when shit went bad with my Pop.

She loved that nigga's dirty drawers, and yet he cheated on her time and time again. He took care of us, but he didn't give a fuck about his woman. Trust and I lay in bed many nights, listening to them fight and hearing her cries after he left. So, that's some shit I'ma stand strong on. I'm sure it's a chick out there that's gone catch my ass slipping, and I'll be ready for her lil ass when that time comes.

True enough Z and I have been fucking around for a little over a year, and I got mad respect for her. She's a dope ass girl, but that doesn't change my feelings or determine if I want to be with her. A nigga has to be mentally ready, and emotionally connected for that type of commitment. Zena was fine as fuck, and the pussy was grade A, and even with all of those qualities, it's still not enough. The one thing I could promise her with is that I would fuck the shit out of her when we were together, and that's it. I handled my hygiene and put my clothes on to leave because this shit sounded like it was about to go left.

"Taj, I'm not trying to be a pain in the ass, and I know what it is with us. I just want more with you, and if you can't give me, that then I'm moving on to a nigga that's gone give me what I need. I'm ready to settle down and get married to a man that loves me just as much as I love him!" She raised her voice, clearly irritated.

"I hope you find that shit, 'cause you deserve it. Let me know where to send a gift." I turned and walked out of her bedroom. What else was I supposed to say to that? She wanted what she wanted.

Chapter Five

TRUST

"We wish you a Merry Christmas...We wish you a Merry Christmas!" This girl is gone make me choke all the Christmas songs outta her ass! This is her second night here, and all her ass been doing is singing and fuckin' screaming! If this is what kidnappers go through. ion want to do this shit no damn more. I haven't heard shit from her nigga about my money, and something is telling me that nigga not coming with my shit.

I haven't had any conversations with her, she asked for food and I made sure she got it. But I was going to be nice and let her come out of the room for a while. Walking down the hall, I opened the door and waited for her to come out. She came in front so that I could see her, and I couldn't believe this damn girl was standing here butt ass naked.

"What the fuck are you doing? Where are your clothes?" I questioned, turning away, trying not to look at how fuckin fine she is.

"Nahhh, look at me! My clothes are where the fuck you left them, in my fucking house! I have nothing, and since you're not going to get me anything to wear. This is how I'm coming, and your ass better not touch me!" She yelled, and I quickly pulled the door shut, locking her in the room. I went down to my mother's room to see if she had any clothes in there. I found a pair of tights and t-shirt for her to put on.

They looked to be about the same size, so I hope she could fit them. I went back down to the room and opened the door to pass her the clothes.

"Put this on, and you can come out of the room." I smiled. She stared at me for a minute with a frown on her face but took the clothes out of my hand. Once she was dressed, she walked out, and we headed downstairs with me.

"What's your name again?" I questioned, looking over at her, really noticing her for the first time. Shorty was a beautiful woman, and now I couldn't understand why she was with Case simple ass.

"Honest... It's Honesty," she stuttered, and I burst into laughter.

"What! What's so damn funny?" She asked, confused at why I was laughing.

"Our names are what's funny. My name is Trust." I laughed again, while she thought about it and then chuckled.

"Are you hungry, Honesty?"

"Yeah, I'm starving." She looked away, fumbling with her hands. This girl looked scared, and nervous, and I swear I felt fucked up about holding her here. I got up and grabbed the iPad off the counter.

"Here, take this and order dinner. All of the restaurants are loaded in there, and I have two credit cards that will automatically populate for you to cash out. Order for the both of us. I'm not difficult; I'll eat whatever you order me. You can order you some clothes, and anything else that you might need on there as well. Hopefully, this will all be over by tomorrow." I smiled over at her.

"Ok." She gave me a half smile.

"Trust, what if he doesn't pay you? What will happen to me?" She asked.

"Let's just focus on the positive; he will pay his debt. How did you end up with a nigga like Case?" I turned to face her.

"I met him four years ago at a party, and we started messing with each other heavy, and a few months later, we were living together. Case helped me during a dark time in my life, and that just made me love him harder. I mean, we don't have a perfect relationship, but who does? Couples go through things, and ours is no different. He said he would always be there for me, and I believe him when he says that. So, I'm sure he's working to get me out of this situation."

I sat here processing everything she was saying, and for her sake, I hope she was right. But I knew that nigga, and Case was nothing more than a fuck up. I knew he was going to fumble this girl's heart and her life. That nigga doesn't give a fuck about nobody, but himself.

"You know your man better than me, baby girl. Look, I gotta run upstairs for minute. Everything is operated by remotes and passcodes. So, please don't think you can just open my doors and leave. I've said this a million times, it seems like, but I promise you I'm not going to hurt you. If you act like you got some sense and stop all that damn Christmas song bullshit, you'll be fine," I told her.

"Why don't you have your Christmas decorations put up? Christmas is the best time of the year, and I'm the happiest during this time. I know this house would look beautiful if it was decorated." She smiled.

"Nah, ion do that Christmas shit up in here," I told her and walked out of the kitchen to go take a quick shower while she placed our order. I hurried and took care of my hygiene, and just as I stepped out of the shower and started drying off, my phone started ringing. I ran to grab it off of my nightstand, and it was Jerry.

"Yeah," I spoke into the phone.

"911 was dialed from the kitchen iPad. Are you good?" He asked.

"That was her; I left her in the kitchen to order dinner. You can send them over." I ended the call and headed back downstairs.

"I ordered some burgers and fries from the steak shop," she nervously stated.

"Burgers sounds good. Did you order some clothes?" I asked, picking up the remote and turning the television on.

"Yeah, I was able to get some things from amazon. Since you have prime, it will be here tomorrow." Just as I was getting ready to respond to her, the doorbell sounded off. I headed for the door, and I put the code in to open the front door. It was two cops standing there.

"Sir, is everything alright? We got a call about a kidnapping happening at this address." He looked past me.

"Everything is good, Officer." I shrugged.

"No, the fuck it's not! Arrest his ass, Officer! He kidnapped me! You going to jail, nigga, and I hope they bury your ass under that bitch! I can't wait to get home and cleanse myself of this bullshit!" She was clapping her hands all in my face with the biggest smile.

"Ma'am, tell your boyfriend to pay boss man his money, and shit like this wouldn't happen to you," Nate told her, and I couldn't help but to give her that same big ass smile she just gave me.

"You never know who's on my payroll, Shorty. Stay woke." I winked at her and she stormed away from the door. All my emergency calls dialed from my home or any of my devices are directed to Jeremy, my tech guy. Once he speaks to me or determines that it's in fact an emergency, he will then call 911. While talking to Nate and Danny, our food arrived. I'm glad because I'm ready for her ass to go back to her room. Walking into my kitchen, she was standing at the counter drinking an apple juice.

"Take your food out of the bag, and let's go!" I gritted. I was trying to be nice to this chick, but she was trying my fuckin patience.

"I'm sorry! I'm scared, and I just wanna go home. I've never been involved in nothing like this before, Trust. Look if sex is what it'll take for you to let me go! Fuck it, I'll do anything to save my life!" She started pulling her clothes off, throwing them at me. I was standing there stuck for a minute, because her body was everything. Normally, I would have jumped at a beautiful naked woman standing in my kitchen. She would've definitely taken the place of my dinner in any other normal situation. But this isn't what I wanted from lil mama.

"Shorty, put your clothes back on. This is not that, and it never will be. I didn't bring you here for sex, to rape you, or kill you!" I pulled her by the arms to lead her back upstairs, and she started swinging on me again. Lifting her into my arms, I forgot her ass was naked, and that shit had my dick hard as fuck. I put her down so damn quick she hit the floor, and she started talking shit.

"This is fucked up! Just let me go home, nigga! Fuck!" I grabbed the bag of food and gave her the iPad to play games on or surf the web. Jerry turned the mobile phone off, so she couldn't send emails, and she wasn't able to go on any social media apps. This girl didn't put her clothes back on. She walked off with all that ass swinging back and forth.

Fuck all that turning away shit. I'm a grown ass man, and if she gone walk her ass around my house like that, then I'ma look. Fuck that! I'm on whatever energy her lil' fine ass is on. I was trying to be a gentleman, but she was definitely about to test my gangsta. It's been an eventful couple of hours. So, I decided to go to bed, and maybe baby girl will get to go home tomorrow.

* * *

Five Days Later

"*I*t's beginning to look a lot like Christmassssss!" I heard singing coming through the intercom, and at this point, I wanted to pull them muthafuckas out the wall. I glanced over at the clock, and it was already a little after the one in the afternoon. I was out a little late last night drinking, and the moment my head hit the pillow, I was out. I've been thinking about letting baby girl go, because this shit really doesn't have shit to do with her, and over the past six days, she's grown on me. It seems that baby girl went through some real shit with both of her parents dying on her at a young age.

She doesn't have much family, and the job that she was bragging about was a job at a local grocery store. Which there was nothing wrong with that, it's the fact that she was willing to work and didn't care where it was just as long as she could provide for herself. That shit was admirable in itself, but baby girl was fucking with me, and as a man I've been doing my best to hold shit together around here.

Day in and night, this girl is walking around this muthafucka naked, and at this point, it doesn't matter if she has clothes; she still going to do it! I think this shit is a game to her at this point. She wants to drive my ass crazy. My brother was right, I definitely didn't think things through with this shit. I can't bring anyone here because she's here. I'm not in a committed relationship, but I do have someone that I fuck with on a regular and I haven't had a chance to get up with her

28

in a while. I've been spending my time here at home, watching over her ass.

Something moving on my balcony caught my attention. I jumped out of bed, grabbed my gun, and slid the door open. It was some dude on a ladder with some damn Christmas lights in his hands.

"What the fuck! What the fuck are you doing on my fuckin' roof?" I questioned with my gun pointed on his ass.

"We were hired to decorate the outside and inside of the house this morning. I'm sorry if we woke you, sir, but we're almost done!" He said to me, and I wanted to push that damn ladder over with his ass on it.

"Get the fuck off my shit!" I roared, and his ass jumped, almost falling off the damn ladder. Walking into the bathroom, I handled my hygiene and headed downstairs 'cause my first question is how did these muthafuckas get on my property and into my gotdamn house!

When I made it downstairs, it looked like my house was turned into some type of magical Christmas theme that you see in magazines, and on television. There were Christmas trees decorated all over the place, in all sizes. It had to be at least fifteen trees so far that I could see. Not to mention the banisters, and other decorative things around the house. How the fuck could I not hear all of this shit going on!

"Heyyyy, buddy! Surprise! Isn't it beautiful in here!" Honesty's cheery, bubbly ass jumped up and down, clapping her hands in excitement.

"How the fuck did they get inside, and what the fuck were you thinking! I didn't order this shit! Who the the fuck are these fuckin' people?! Get the fuck out! Get out of my shit right now, before I let off in this muthafucka!" I roared, and the designers started scattering around the room, grabbing their shit. A few minutes later, they were out the door.

"Ohhhhhhhhh, this is nicccceeeee!" I heard my grandmother say sounding like Tiffany damn Haddish. I dropped my damn head, knowing her and Taj's messy asses were coming over to fuck with me. They called me every damn day asking about Honesty ass. Madear talking 'bout they wanted to make sure the cops hadn't raided me yet.

"It's real...real...real Christmassy in here! That nigga must've woken up and forgot all about him hating Christmas," Taj said to her. Honesty walked her half-dressed ass out into the foyer, and I followed behind her shaking my damn head.

"Hi!" She smiled.

"Damnnn! Bro-Bro got him a bad one! Sup, shorty." Taj smiled at her, licking his damn lips.

"We came over to check on hostage central, but she must be locked away since you got company... Oopps, my bad! I wasn't supposed to say that you holding people hostage... Ohhh shit, let me just shut the fuck up. I haven't had my weed yet, so I'm not thinking with a high mind." Madear shook her head.

"Yeah, 'cause fuckin' with you, this nigga gone be in jail by tonight," Taj told her.

"Ummmm, I'm the hostage. Since you all know that I've been here, it's no use in asking you to help me leave. Besides, I kind of like it here now, and my friend Trust here is kinda cool." She smiled, patting me on my shoulder. Madear and Taj looked at each other then back to us.

"Uhhhh... that's how they doing kidnappings now in the US of A?" Madear asked, looking all damn confused.

"This the same chick? 'Cause she damn sure didn't look like that when we got her ass... Fuck! I mean, when you got her ass. For the record, this nigga kidnapped you on his own. It's amazing what a comb, a lil' water, soap, makeup, and clothes can do." Taj laughed.

"Y'all gotta go. I got some shit to handle here." I walked them both outside, and when I saw all of the shit in my yard and the decorations on my house, I almost swing on her ass!

"Fuckkkkkkk!" I felt like I was about to damn explode. This fuckin' girl got a fuckin' Ferris wheel on my damn property with Santa, Rudolph, Gifts, a damn Snowman and some other bullshit inside.

"What's wrong?" Madear questioned.

"This! This girl is driving my ass crazy. She's the one that ordered all of this bullshit! Taj, I need for you and Saud to go pull up on Case ass NOW! This nigga is playing, and I'm ready to send his bitch ass to hang out with Mike and his mama," I spat.

"I got you." He dapped me up, and I said my goodbyes to both of them, looking up at the house, and all of the decorations again. Honesty was standing on her balcony naked waving at me! This shit had to stop! Fuckkkk! Just as I was about to walk inside the house, a FedEx and Amazon truck was driving up the driveway. I didn't order anything in a while unless my mama placed some orders for me.

"Sup?" I spoke, waiting on the package. These niggas both started unloading box after box, after fuckin' box on my steps and in front of my damn house.

"Sir, I have one large box. Do you think you can help me with this one?" The Amazon guy asked me, and I looked at that nigga like he had three fuckin' heads.

"Nigga, fuck you and that box!" I roared, ready to knock him and them fuckin' packages back on the truck.

"I got you, bruh!" The FedEx driver told him. And when this nigga pulled the big ass 95-inch television off the truck, I almost lost my shit. I knew damn well I didn't order any of this shit. Pulling my phone out, I dialed my mom's number.

"Hey, baby. I've been meaning to call you about Christmas dinner. I wanted to know if we could have dinner at your house this year? The contractor said they won't be finished in time." She sighed. I hate telling my mom no, but she knew how I felt about Christmas.

"Mom, let's talk about that later. Did you place an order and have everything shipped here?" I asked her.

"No, I didn't send anything over there. What's wrong?" She questioned with concern.

"Nothing, I just got a package, and I didn't order it. Let me call you back." I ended the call. Honesty came outside, jumping up and down, and started carrying the boxes in the house.

"What are you doing? We need to send this shit back. I didn't order any of this shit!" I took the box out of her hands and sat it down.

"Yeah, you kinda did order it. Well, technically, I ordered it, but I got some stuff for you too. Since Christmas is coming, Grinches deserve a present too, I guess. See, your name is on all of the packages, and why yo' mama named you that ugly ass name Cleothis?! On God! I would never admit to having that shit as a middle name. I would change everything to Trust C. Williams. If somebody asks you what the C stands for, please lie because you can't be a boss nigga walking around talking about Cleothis." She laughed.

"Fuckkkkkk!" I turned to walk out of the family room, knocking one of the damn Christmas trees over on my way out. I wanted to choke the life out of this girl. All that shit she ordered had me ready to smoke her ass. From what I could see, there were two iPads, two iMacs, shit from Louis Vuitton, Gucci, Fendi; I even saw a package from Hermes. And God knows what she ordered from Amazon. It had to be every bit of fifty to seventy-five boxes down there. Pulling up my credit card charges, I had to sit here for a minute to control my breathing.

"I'ma kill this bitch!"

Chapter Six

HONESTY

I've been sitting here on cloud fucking nine! I knew he would lose his shit when he saw his house decorated and all the shit I've ordered off his credit cards. When I found out that I could just order anything, and the card would populate when it was time to pay, ohhh babbby, I went in on that man's shit! He was better off fucking with Case than me. My plan is to drive his fine ass crazy, and that shit was working. I was about to bite down on my chicken sandwich, when I felt myself being snatched in the air, and my fuckin' sandwich went flying all over the place.

"You think this shit a game! Your lil' swiping ass bought two hundred thousand fuckin' dollars worth of shit! Are you fuckin' crazy?!" He yelled, holding the gun to my head and what my crazy ass did next. He was so mad his eyes were bloodshot red, his gaze never left mine though, and I couldn't look away. The buildup was driving me crazy. It was so bad that I started grinding my body against his arms. I've been doing my best to drive his ass crazy, but I had to stay away from him because of this very reason

. I wanted to fuck the shit out of this man, and I know it's bad because he took my ass and I just met him. But I wanted him, and I wanted to be a hoe just once in my life. Don't judge me, judge your

33

mammy! All Case ass does is cheat on me. It doesn't make it right, but it'll make me feel good for the time being.

"Fuck me!" I moaned.

"I will shred your little ass apart in here, Shorty! Don't walk into some shit you can't get out of!" He gritted, biting down on his bottom lip.

"Fuck me!" I could feel the fire rising inside of me, and the moment I slid my tongue across his lips, he sucked my tongue into his mouth, damn near suffocating me. We both fought to get our clothes off, and in no time, he was entering me without a second thought. My pussy was dripping wet for this man. His deep strokes were lethal. As he thrusted in and out of me at a rapid pace, and all I could do was to hold on and cry out. He pounded on my pussy so good, I could barely remember my damn name.

"Ohhh fuck!" I cried out, as he slammed into me over and over again.

"This what you wanted, right! You've been walking around fucking with me all week with this beautiful ass body. You wanted this dick, and you gone take all of this muthafucka! You not gone keep walking around my shit thinking I won't knock these fuckin' walls down! Fuck-kkk!" He gritted, and it was the way this nigga was talking to me that had my pussy on go. His deep strokes went deeper, and deeper. I tried my best to throw this pussy on him, but he was on beast mode. Sex is always good when tensions are high, and you got a fine ass, big dick nigga fucking you senseless.

"Fuck! I can't take this dick!" I moaned as I held onto him.

"You gone take all of this dick, shorty," he growled, fucking the shit out of me.

"Trust!" I cried, cumming all over his dick. He was pounding the fuck out of me so hard I could feel his dick pulsating like it had its own damn heartbeat.

"Got damn! This some good, wet ass pussy! Fuckkkk!" He roared as he released inside of me. We tried to catch our breath for a few minutes before he pulled out of me. He stood there in his own thoughts, and I knew the realization of what we had just done hit him.

"My bad, this shouldn't have went down like that! Fuck!" He helped me down from the counter and walked out of the kitchen. I was standing there confused about what had just happened. The sex wasn't planned; it just happened. He's right, though. It was probably a mistake, and I wish at this point that he would just let me go home. I went upstairs to my room so that I could shower and put on some clothes. A couple of hours later, I was starving and headed back downstairs to try to eat again, hoping that his fine ass would come in and do a replay of what happened earlier.

"So, this nigga just doesn't give a fuck that his girl is with me?" I heard Trust ask someone. I just stood on the staircase 'cause I couldn't tell if he was on the phone or talking to someone until they started talking, and it was his brother.

"If we didn't press that nigga about your money, we wouldn't have gotten it. That nigga got another bitch, and they kid up in that house. She fine as fuck, so I guess if you trying to hit. you can," his brother said to him.

"Nah, I'm good on that." Hearing Trust say that stung a little bit. But hearing them say that Case had another girl, and a kid sucker punched me in the chest. That nigga didn't give a damn if I was hurt or not! Fuck him! The doorbell going off jolted me from my thoughts.

"Sir, we have a car delivery up front at the gate," his security guard spoke, and I held my hand over my mouth. I forgot I ordered that damn Mercedes off of his credit card. To be honest, I didn't think it would go through, but it did.

"A fuckin' car!" He roared. I could hear the truck in the driveway, and they started unloading it. Trust and his brother was outside talking to his security and the delivery people.

"Why you buy that lil' ass shit?" His brother questioned. But Trust came rushing into the house and ran into me on the staircase.

"That's it! It's time for you to go! Go get your things! You're free to leave." He was pissed, and I was a little hurt by his attitude.

"Trust, I'm sorry. I only did all of this to get back at you for taking me. I wanted to go home, and I felt like driving you crazy and pissing you off enough that you would let me go," I told him.

"You're right! You can go and take as much of this shit with you as you can!"

"What about what just happened?" I looked over at him.

"Act like it didn't happen. Taj, help her get this shit out of here. She can have whatever she can take with her." Is all he said before he walked away, and that shit hurt my feelings. I didn't take all of the things I ordered, but I didn't have a dime to my name or a job anymore. I know they fired me, and this nigga didn't even give a fuck about that. I told his brother I didn't need any help, just as long as I could take the car. He double checked with his brother, and he said that I could have the car. When I bought the car, I put it in my name and just paid for it with his card. This car and the things were a blessing to me for sure, because my car was on its last leg. Even though I went through this shit, I will say nothing about it was bad. I was just scared at first because a stranger was taking me, but who wouldn't be scared.

I went straight to the house I shared with Case. I had a lot to say to that nigga and I prayed he still had his bitch there. I had so much shit in the car, I could barely see out of the damn window and prayed nobody robbed my ass. Even though Trust didn't hurt me, things could have gone really bad if he was that type of nigga. Case bitch ass was going to leave me there.

I got out of the car and walked to the door. I didn't have my key, and the door was locked, so I had no choice but to knock on the door and cover the peephole.

"Who is it?" Some girl asked, and I didn't say a word hoping she would open the door. Seconds later. the door flew open, and I pushed my way right on in.

"What the hell!" She screamed until she noticed who I was, because I damn sure knew who she was.

"So, you in here playing house with my nigga, bitch!" I spat, slapping the fuck out of her. I done beat her ass before over this no good ass nigga. Normally I wouldn't go at a bitch that didn't know I existed, but this bitch knew who the fuck I was.

"Caseee!" She yelled, and his dumb ass came running down the stairs with his gun.

"Shit! Hey, ba...babe...Damn, I'm glad that nigga let you go. I tried to come up with the money sooner, but I met up with him and gave him your shit. He said he was gone let you go when he was ready." He smiled, trying to pull me in for a hug.

"So, this how we doing it? You gone just keep fucking with these bum bitches?!" I snapped, jumping in his face.

"You ain't shit, nigga! I knew you were still fucking with this bitch!" I slapped the shit out of his ass.

"Daddy!" The little boy cried behind them, and I spazzed the fuck out.

"Daddy! So that was your baby this bitch was carrying!" I yelled with tears streaming down my face.

"You not gone keep calling me to many more bitches, bitch!" I jumped clean across the room and beat that bitch ass. She knew what it was, which is why her ass was standing so far away. But if I want to get yo' ass, I'm gone get at you. It doesn't matter where the fuck you are.

"Honesty! Stop that shit, my son is watching you hurt his mama." Hearing that nigga call him his son caused me to start swinging on his ass. I took too much from this nigga in the past four years, and enough was enough! I ran upstairs and started grabbing all of my important shit that I needed, making sure to get my computer and phone.

"Where the fuck are you going? I know I be fuckin' up sometimes, but you know damn well it's all about you. She's just something to do, babe. I have to be there for them because she got my son. I didn't admit to it because I knew you would leave me. You know I love you, and I can't do this shit without you." He tried to grab me, I punched his ass again, and he grabbed my arms.

"Cut that shit out, babe! I'ma stop cheating on you, I promise." This nigga had the nerve to look like he was sincere.

"You don't have to stop cheating, 'cause the dick I got from your boss! Was definitely boss status! It was the best dick I ever had in my life. A nigga like you could fuckin' never!" I smirked and turned to get the rest of my shit.

"Bitch, you fucked that nigga! I'ma kill yo' ass!" He roared, jumping into my face., and he was met with my nine.

"Worry about the bitch you got a kid with," I said, grabbing my shit and walking out. I didn't know where I was going, but it was time

I got the fuck away from this place. My cousin has been trying to get me to come stay with her, and for years I've been turning my nose up at the idea because of Case's ass. I didn't have anything holding me back now. Winter Crest here I come, and I pray things start to look up for me there.

Chapter Seven

TRUST

*I*t's been a few days, and I'm still pissed about ole girl ordering all this shit. Half of the shit is still here because she couldn't take all of it with her. I was planning to have the rest of it delivered to her tomorrow. I never expected for things to get out of hand with her, and I damn sure didn't expect to fuck her. I was pissed, tensions were high, and shorty had a way of getting my attention.

I'm a man first, and you not gone keep throwing pussy, and ass in my face, and I not react. Shit was crazy, and even though she had me ready to choke the shit out of her lil feisty fine ass, she's been on my mind since she left. The last couple of nights I've had to stop myself from going to pull her out of that nigga's bed. That's what type of time I'm on, and when I'm on that shit, it's hard as fuck to come down from it. In a week's time lil mama left a lasting impression with her credit card swiping ass.

I had to laugh at the shit 'cause lil baby went ham on my ass and bought a damn car. Where they do that shit at? A fuckin car! I'm not sure what was going on, but I miss seeing her walking around butt ass naked trying to send my ass to the crazy house. I hope shit is good on the home front with her and Case dumb ass. I can't believe that nigga did her like that. If I didn't have Taj run down on his ass, he was going to take his time paying what he owed me and leave her with me not knowing if she was in real danger, and that was fucked up. I hope she wakes up and realizes that she deserves so much more. Dealing with that nigga, had me questioning myself daily because in any other situation, his bitch ass would be dead.

It's taking everything in me not to disrespect my homie and honor his wishes. That shit was hard as fuck, but that nigga gonna keep pushing me and it's gone be lights out for his bitch ass.

Tonight, I'm throwing a party for my crew at Saud's bar 215 to show my appreciation and give bonuses for all they've done for me and our organization during the year. I've always taken care of my crew and made sure they were good during the holidays. This shit didn't just start now. It's something I've done for years, so it was hard to understand why Von turned on me.

That shit fucked with me because that was my nigga a hundred grand. I would've done anything for him. And the same for Saud. Those were my brothers. If they came to me asking for more money at any point in time, they would've gotten it. I have never been a selfish nigga, and I'll always look out for the ones I love. My phone ringing jolted me out of my thoughts.

"Sup?" I answered.

"Are you on your way?" Taj asked.

"Pulling in front of the bar now," I replied.

"Bet. I'll see you in a minute." He ended the call. I pulled up in front of the bar and got out of the car. Tonight will be the first time I've seen Case since the shit went down with his girl. All I know is that nigga better tread lightly 'cause my trigger finger been itching since he started working for me. I made my way over to our section in VIP, and the crew had the bottles flowing. Just as the bottle girl poured my drink, Saud came walking into the section with a girl on his arms, and it damn sure wasn't Shantay.

"What up, this is my friend Stacia. Bae, these are my brothers, Trust and Taj," Saud introduced.

"Nah, nigga, take your ass down on the main level with all that new girl shit. Ain't nobody got time for Shantay crazy ass. And damn sure don't want the bullet that's meant for you and her ass to hit me. I still got too much living and pussy to get," Taj told him, and I fell out laughing because Taj was right. Shantay's ass was certified.

"Shantay on that shit, and I'm getting tired of the back and forth with her ass. One minute we together, and the next minute, she on that we need space bullshit. So, I'm giving her ass space. I need me a lil shorty to wrap gifts with for Christmas." This nigga laughed, pouring his girl a drink.

"Wrap gifts with! Nigga, you and her ass gone definitely be wrapped if you keep playing Shantay ass." Taj was a damn fool, but I had to agree with him yet again. Case came walking in with some chick, and it sure in the fuck wasn't Honesty. These niggas were on demon time. What the fuck was in the air? Damn sure not no Holiday Cheer.

"Look at this slow nigga, and I don't know if I'm going blind or not but from the looks of it, that ain't Hostage with him," Taj stated.

"Nah, that's not her. At all. That look like the girl that was at the crib when we picked the money up," Saud told him.

"Sure is, and that nigga dumb as fuck 'cause Hostage is the mutha-fuckin' package. This chick looks like a malnutrition duck, the fuck wrong with her lips?"

"What's up?" Case spoke, walking up with a frown on his face, dapping Taj and Saud up. He didn't speak to me, and the nigga had the nerve to mug me. I had to laugh to keep from bustin' this nigga in his shit.

"Nigga, the fuck wrong with you?!" Taj asked him.

"This nigga my problem! I just came to get my bonus; I don't have shit to say to none of y'all niggas. This nigga come up in my shit, take my girl, and then bust her down. Fuck you niggas!" He spat, and my gun was out and on him before he could say another fuckin word.

"Who the fuck you talking to, nigga! Did you think I would deny the shit? If you know, that means she told you! And the fact that you're bringing your ass in here on so rah-rah shit like you gone do somethin' is funny as fuck to me. Nigga, nothing about your existence scares me. Yeah, I fucked your girl! I was so deep in her wet ass pussy; my dick touched her fuckin' soul and sketched my name all over that muthafucka.

The only regret I have about fucking her is sending her back to your pussy ass. Don't come up in here acting like you that nigga 'cause bitch, I will make you eat these fuckin' bullets and end your life! Stop fuckin' playing with me!" I gritted in his face.

"Damn, this nigga took your girl out yo' bed, just told you he had so much dick up in her, her soul is his now, and you just got a shell. Her soul, nigga?! You know how much dick a nigga gotta have to do some shit like that? Nah, you still a straight bitch, cause niggggggaaaa, this dude just put dick all up in yo' girl, and you just standing there mean mugging the nigga!

Do you know how many bullets that nigga would've done ate if he told me some shit like that! Allum! And nigga, I can't believe you was over there slanging dick all up and through Hostage. As fine as her ass is though, I would've done the same thing!" Taj laughed, shaking his head. This nigga was always instigating and talking shit when it came to this nigga.

"Nigga, fuck y-" Was all he could get the fuck out before I was on his ass. I had so much aggression to get out, and I'ma give it all to this nigga. His bitch ass should have been got this work and a muthafuckin' bullet. I was so pissed I was ready to bury this nigga! Saud pulled me off of his bitch ass because Taj was gone let me beat this nigga to sleep. That's just how me and my brother was with it. If we were beating a niggas ass, let us do that shit until we stopped or that nigga was dead. It's one or the other, no in between.

"He's fuckin' out! That nigga can't eat off my muthafuckin' table, and if I see you niggas fuckin' with him, yo' ass won't eat off my shit either! Nigga, if you even breathe my way, I'ma kill you. That's the only warning you gone get from me!" I roared, running up on him and smashing my gun against his head. Saud had some of the guys get him out of the bar while his girl screamed and cried. I made sure I paid everyone their bonuses and ended my night early because I was ten seconds from going back to that nigga crib and pulling Honesty ass up outta there.

After I calmed a little, I decided to leave baby girl alone. I've put her through alot and disrupted her life enough. I just hope one day she wakes up and moves on from that lame ass nigga.

Christmas was coming, and my mom wanted us to give out food vouchers and gifts to families in need for the holidays. Even though it's not my favorite time of the year, I'll never disappoint her because there were times where we didn't have it, or she couldn't buy gifts for us during the Christmas season. I'm a ruthless nigga, but my heart is big, and I would hate for a kid to wake up and not have any gifts under their tree. So, Taj and I will always be down to do whatever she needs us to do. It was time for me to get my head back to where it was before I snatched Honesty's sleepy ass out of her house. The pussy was immaculate, and her company would be missed, but she chose that nigga, and I had to live with that.

* * *

Ten Months Later

*T*oday is my mom's birthday, and I'm on my way over because I heard Madear was over there cooking fried fish, shrimp, and crabs. Once I got the word, I hurried and got my ass up. One thing my mom and grandmother could do is cook, and me and Taj was gone always show up to eat. His ass was the one that called me and told me she was cooking. Twenty minutes later, I was pulling into my mom's driveway and heading into the house. Just as I turned to close the door, a black Suburban pulled into the driveway.

"Who is that?" Taj asked, walking up to see who these white dudes getting out of the truck were.

"I don't know. Are you dirty?" I asked, looking over at him.

"I'm Gucci." I opened the door to see what these dudes wanted. I hope they ass wasn't them folk trying to shake me down. I already got enough of they snake asses on my payroll.

"Sup?" I asked.

"Hello, we're looking for Regina Williams," one of the guys spoke.

"Who the hell are you, and what do you need with Regina?" I asked him.

"My name is attorney Jason Strayer, and I would like to speak to her about an old acquaintance of hers, Mr. Armon Crest."

"Armon Crest? Ma doesn't know nobody named Armon," Taj stated.

"Who is at the door?" Ma questioned, coming into the living room.

"Some attorney. He said he wanna talk to you about a dude named Armon," Taj told her, and she looked on in surprise. Almost like her ass was in shock and couldn't form a word to speak.

"Mom, you good?" I asked her because now I was concerned.

"Ye...yeah. Let them in," she advised, and we stepped aside so that they could come inside.

"Hi, I'm Regina Williams. How can I help you?" She asked in confusion.

"Regina, Jason Strayer. These are my colleagues, Devin Smith, and Jared Arlington we're the attorneys that represent Armon Crest III. Mr. Crest passed away last month, and he left us a note to locate you on claims that you share an illegitimate child with Mr. Crest," he said to her.

"Ahhh hell, shit 'bout to get hectic in here. Taj, light us a blunt 'cause we all gone need that shit in about ten minutes," Madear blurted, taking a seat.

"Ma, what is he talking about? Who's Armon Crest?" I questioned.

"Um... He's your father, Trust. I'm confused about all of this; he denied my son, and I left it at that. So, why now? If he's dead, why are you all here bothering us?" She asked, and that was good fuckin' question because fuck that dude living or dead.

"Mr. Crest was the sole heir of the Crest family and the city of Winter Crest, Pa. If your son is in fact his son, then he now becomes the sole heir to the Crest empire, and the city of Winter Crest," he stated, and I swear we were all sitting here with our mouths hanging opened.

"What the fuck is a Winter Crest? I've lived in Philly all my life and I have never heard of the city, town, or whatever the fuck it is before," Taj explained. He was looking just as puzzled as we all were.

"Winter Crest is one of the most beautiful quaint cities in Pennsylvania. If you don't mind, may we please sit? I have a document here and the letter from Armon, you can read it all. Are you the child in question?" He asked Taj.

"Hell to the nawl! I know my pappy, but if this nigga done left my brother a damn city? I can trade with him and take this rich dead nigga! Trust my Pop not gone mind at all 'cause in the end we gone all be rich." Taj dumb ass didn't care what he said out of his mouth.

"You better let'em know!" Madear blurted.

"My son Trust is the child in questioned." My mom pointed to me, and he turned in my direction.

"Trust, it's nice to meet you, sir. Here are the write-ups on Winter Crest and how it all got started. It'll probably be better if you read this versus me explaining it to you. I could go on and on about our thriving city." He handed me the document, and I sat and read it aloud, so that my family could hear about it as well. This shit is crazy as hell and I'm confused just as everyone else, but if reading this paper was going to shed some insight, I was for it.

The city of Winter Crest, Pennsylvania, was re-established on Christmas Eve of 1946 when the Crest family stumbled on the small town. Upon discovery, it was at that time named Maple Valley. Armon Crest was a business developer that saw the potential Maple Valley possessed and felt he could bring this little town to life. It was his dream to own housing developments, but never in his wildest dreams did he think he could acquire a town. Armon spent countless hours and restless nights researching to find a way to obtain the lands in Maple Valley. It wasn't until a few years later, the opportunity to purchase Maple Valley landed on his desk, and he immediately jumped into action. A few months later, Armon became the sole owner of the town.

Before Armon was granted ownership, he'd already planted seeds in the small town. He knew every slope, plot, and field, and the ideas for what he wanted to do with the land were perfectly planned. As the new owner of Maple Valley, he slowly began making changes; One of those changes was the town's name. Armon and his wife Carolyn birthed two children; a daughter and a son. Winter and Armon Jr. were his motivation for dreaming big. The Crests were big on family, and being that Armon re-established the land on Christmas Eve, which was also his eldest child's birthday, made good for their holiday cheer. Armon loved his blonde hair blue-eyed children, but his daughter Winter was his prize possession. Polio claimed Winter's life months before Armon scored the town. Armon decided that he wanted to honor his first child, so Maple Valley became Winter Crest.

Armon wanted to evolve Winter Crest into something no one had ever seen. The town as it stood wasn't fitting for his plans. Armon didn't just want a small town; he wanted it to be a thriving city. Armon wanted his city to keep its natural beauty but be a place where people could thrive. He wanted people to be able to love his city enough to where they desired to live and raise their families. The more he daydreamed about Winter Crest, the more he brought his visions to life. After years of development, Winter Crest became one of the most beautiful places to live.

The city has had its ups and downs throughout the decades, overpopulation being one of them. The urban community claimed over 30% of the population and has become an intricate part of the growing city. Armon is most proud of the diversity that ignites his city, and his once small town now features a wide range of ethnicities. As in many cities around the world fight with poverty, Winter Crest isn't exempt from that as well. Armon fought hard to make sure there were working opportunities for all, but not everyone was fortunate enough to live without struggle. Instead of closing out his pride and joy to newcomers, Armon bought more land and expanded to meet the needs of all that wanted to settle in his gorgeous city.

Winter Crest is home of several fortune five hundred companies, creating jobs and opportunities for its residents. The city has the perfect balance of nature and city life with its clearwater lakes, peaked mountains, lengthy wooded trails, Skyscraper buildings, award-winning restaurants, one of the best Trauma and Children's Hospitals in the nation, and the best Award-winning law firms in the North. Vacations are a must in Winter Crest as it nests many hotels, but the largest resort-style, aesthetically pleasing, and five-star hotel owned by the Crest Family.

Since the city was purchased during Christmas Eve, which was also Winter's birthday, people travel far and wide to participate in the city's annual Holiday Festival. The Snowy weather always set the tone for the Christmas season. The festival takes place at city hall and features traditional dishes, games, a toy drive, and a concert. Winter Crest doesn't just celebrate Xmas; every holiday, the city celebrates with free food, fireworks, live entertainment, and giveaways. Suppose you're looking for a place with tolerable weather every season, job placement, schools that test amongst the highest in the nation, and magnificent subdivisions featured on HGTV. In that case, Winter Crest is where you want to live. There are several businesses that are marked as thriving staples in the city of Winter Crest and urban communities of the city.

I couldn't even form in words what I wanted to say after reading this document.

"Uhhhhh, did you say blonde hair blue eyed children?! So, my nigga not really a nigga? So, nigga, you a damn caramel latte! I knew something was up with your ass with all that damn fine baby hair, them damn eyes, and that funny-looking complexion. Ma, so mookie and nem wasn't the only niggas in your Rolodex? You had an array of choices, huh? Madear, you're right. I think we need to smoke that blunt because this shit about to get real interesting." Taj looked over at me, and I looked at my mom for answers.

"Ma, you need to talk to me about this. All you've ever said is that the dude wanted nothing to do with us. How did this happen? Is this guy really my dad?" I asked her.

"Hell yeah, he your daddy! Did you hear all the shit he owned? In my eyes that equates to rich and rich as fuck at that!" my mom nudged my brother, and stood from her seat.

"Can you all excuse us for a second? Trust, can I talk to you in private for a minute?" She grabbed my hand and pulled me into the kitchen.

"Ma, is this real? I'm so confused right now; my Pop was a white man?" I couldn't believe what was going on right now. I don't have anything to do with white people at all, but I never knew the guy was a white man. I knew that I looked different from my brother, mom, and grandmother, but for some reason, I never expected this.

"Son, I met him at a conference for my job. He was the guest speaker, we were all staying at the same hotel, and he and I ended up in the same restaurant one night. We were both eating alone, and started drinking, getting to know one another. And in our drunkenness, we ended up in bed together. After that night, we didn't say much to each other. Once the conference was over, he went his way, and I went mine.

Two months later, I was hit with the surprise of my life. I found out I was pregnant with you. I knew who he was of course, and I reached out to him. As to be expected, he didn't remember much about our night together because he was so drunk. He was engaged to be married and said he couldn't allow this to get out. He didn't want this to interfere with his life. I ended the call right then and there and never reached out to him again, and he never came looking for us.

He was rich and powerful; I didn't want to bring problems to us in any kind of way, so I just left it alone. I know Armon Crest III is your father. I've never been sure about anything in my life. If they say you're the sole heir of his empire, you go get what's yours by any means necessary. I know you're stubborn and may say you don't want anything from him, but if you're the only living heir, God only knows where that money will go. Let's just hear them out and see what they want you to do." She gave me a half smile.

My brother's pops treated me like I was his my entire life, and even though he wasn't shit to my mama as far as a partner, he was good to us. I wasn't looking for a daddy. Dead or alive. I'm having shit in real life, and although I don't own cities and shit, I'm doing well for myself. I really didn't want shit from this Armon character, but I could feel how important this was to my mom. If she wanted me to go get what was mine, then that's what it was.

"Ok." I stood from my seat and went back out to see what my next steps were.

"Where do we go from here?" I asked.

"We'll need for you to come to Winter Crest as soon as possible. Of course, we will have to do a DNA to determine paternity and confirm Mr. Crest's and your mother's claims. Once that's done, we will start the legal proceedings for you to take possession of the Crest Estate. My team is headed back to the hotel to gather our things. Our private jet is set to leave Philadelphia this evening 7 p.m. You and your family are more than welcome to join us, so that we can get things underway," he stated, and I knew I needed to go but hated to leave because it was my mom's birthday.

"I'm going with you, bro," Taj assured me.

"We're all going with you, baby. You don't have to face this alone." My mom grabbed my hand and I felt more at ease.

"We'll see you at 7. But one more thing, exactly how much is the Crest estate worth?" I asked, and he opened the file he was holding.

"Roughly 10.7 billion." He smiled, and my knees buckled. 10.7 fucking billion? A nigga like me didn't even know what all that money meant. I almost passed the fuck out.

"Shit!" Taj blurted.

"Whewwww, babbbyyy! We need to hurry up and get to Mayberry before these fortune (fortunate) people change their damn minds." Madear jumped up, grabbing her purse, and walked out the door.

"Yeah, we'll meet you all at the airport. Can you send the information that we need so that we know where to go once we get there?" I shook their hands, and they left out.

"What the fuck just happened? Mom!" I looked at her in disbelief. If this was true, my ass had just become a billionaire at 28. I couldn't believe this shit. A whole fucking billionaire? Me? All that money was mine? I really couldn't believe this was actually happening.

"I know, son. I can't believe this shit myself. At least he didn't die without acknowledging that you existed. That shit must have eaten at him, and I'm happy as hell that he thought about you in the end." She cried, pulling me into a hug, and I swear I cried with her. Just thinking about our struggles, and all the shit she had to endure as a single mother because she didn't have the help she needed.

If he would've accepted me as his child, I wouldn't have had to go through what I did, even in the streets. My life could have been different. I'm certain that it would have been. We all agreed to meet up at my house, and I would have a service take us to the airport. I called Saud to let him know what was going on, and he couldn't believe what the hell was going on either. I wanted him to stay behind to make sure shit was running smooth here, and I would let him know when he could come out. It was a little after 3 and I had a lot of things to do before we left. My phone started ringing, and it was Taj calling.

"Sup, bro?" I picked up on the first ring.

"I was just checking to see if we were still billionaires before I packed up all my shit and dropped it off down in the hood for these niggas to have! 'Cause a nigga 'bout to get tailored made 'errthang!" He laughed.

"Nigga! Get the fuck off my damn phone."

My brother already knew if I was a billionaire then so was he.

What was mine is his. It wasn't shit my brother couldn't get from me. Hell, my whole family was set for life behind this shit. I already took care of my people but I was about to turn this shit up a couple notches. A nigga had a whole empire literally.

"Aht aht! You gone have to chill out on that nigga shit. Nigga, you not a hundred percent nigga, and we don't play that shit. I guess I need to know which side you operating off of before you use that term. It's definitely giving me your other side right now. I'ma need to know if you're speaking from your white perspective or your black perspective, and that determines if yo' ass can use the word nigga, nigga!" I had to look at my phone for minute, and then I hung up on his crazy ass. Cause nigga, what!

I started packing my things, and once I was done with that, I went down to speak with my security team 'bout me leaving for a while. Before I knew it, my family had arrived, and it was time for us to leave. I'm not sure what was in store for me, but I knew my life was getting ready to change forever.

A few hours later, we had landed in Winter Crest and were on our way to the Elixar Hotel, Resort & Spa to get settled in. From what I could see, this city was beautiful, and it looks as if it would be my new home for a while. I don't know what I was expecting, maybe a small country town, but seeing the tall buildings, beautiful lakes, and busy city life had me in awe. This shit was almost futuristic looking. I'd spotted a few award-winning restaurants I couldn't wait to try that I'd heard of but didn't know where they were in Pennsylvania. This place was gorgeous and I couldn't believe it was all mine.

Chapter Eight

HONESTY

*O*ne Week Later:
Life has a way of beating you down, and it's definitely tearing my ass up. My cousin has been such a blessing to me, but it's been hard as hell for me. I was able to find me a job almost immediately at the Elixar Hotel as a housekeeper until I got really sick. I was unable to work for over a week, and got fired. I was so sick I ended up in the emergency room, and I found out that I was two months pregnant. I was in shock because I was still getting my cycle. The only thing that was off with me was the fact that I got so sick. I mean, I couldn't get out of bed, and it was like that through my entire pregnancy.

I had so many emotions going on because I wasn't ready for a child, and I damn sure didn't want to have one with Case. There were so many times I contemplated on an abortion, but decided against it. I kept telling myself that I opened my legs to get pregnant, so I was going to open them to have this baby. My mom would've been so excited to have a grandchild. I miss her so much. My dad was shot and killed when I was five, and my mom died from Breast cancer when I was a junior in high school. That shit broke me because I couldn't move on from losing her.

My mom was my everything, and not having her killed my spirits. The reason I love Christmas so much is because that was her favorite time of the year. We would always make cookies, drink eggnog and hot chocolate, and watch Christmas movies. She said she was raised with her mom putting nuts, oranges, and candy in a brown paper bag because they couldn't afford stockings. So, she did that for me, and even though I had a stocking, she put some of the same things that she had when she was my age in my stocking, and that meant so much to me. When she died, I went to stay with my aunt Sylvia, and my cousin Mena. Having Case in my life took my mind away from all of the stresses of the world. I thought he was good for me, until I moved in with him and our sugar went to shit. My phone ringing pulled me from my thoughts.

"Hello."

"What's up, beautiful? You got everything you need for tomorrow?" Rob asked.

"Yeah, I'm just trying to get things situated for Oshea. I just hope I'm not moving too soon; Oshea is only a month old." I sighed.

"You'll be fine, baby girl. Come hang with a nigga for a minute and let me rub on that fine ass booty." I could hear the smile in his voice.

"I can't tonight. Mena isn't here, and I need to get some rest for tomorrow," I told him. We spoke for a few minutes longer and then ended the call. I got up to iron my clothes and lay everything out so that I could be on time in the morning. I was hired at Winter Crest General Hospital as a receptionist, and I start tomorrow morning. I had to go back to work. I needed money to take care of my baby. I sold most of the things Trust let me have, and that's what I lived off of, but I still have the car. I know I was bullshitting and trying to drive him crazy when I ordered the car, but I'm so glad I have it to get around.

Thank God for my cousin and my friend Rob. They're both helping me out, and I'm so damn grateful. I met Rob when I first moved to Winter Crest. He was a street dude, and it was just something about a dude from the streets that always get me. I didn't know I was pregnant when I met him, and a month after I moved here, we had sex. I knew the baby wasn't his because when I got sick, I was already eight weeks.

I couldn't sleep with him again, knowing that I was carrying another man's baby, and he respected my wishes. He's been so supportive through my pregnancy and was at the hospital when I had my baby. Of course, he wasn't in the delivery room, but he was in the waiting area the whole time. My cousin Mena only has a one-bedroom townhouse in Cabrini Heights, and now that I have the baby, things are getting tight. So, I knew I would have to move soon.

I've thought about reaching out to Oshea's father so many times, and the fact that I'm so afraid of his rejection is the only reason I haven't. My entire pregnancy I assumed my baby was Case's child, until he was born and came out looking like an exact replica of the man that's invaded my mind for months. The situation between us was definitely different, so I'm not sure how to even approach him. I know that I have to do it, and I will at some point. But right now, I had to figure out how to get things on track for me and my son. My phone beeped to let me know that a text message was coming through.

Case: *You know the cops still looking for you. You made my girl lose her baby and you gone pay for that shit.*

This nigga texted me a few days after I left him, talking about his bitch pressed charges on me, and as soon as the cops find me, I'm going to jail. Fuck him and his bitch! He's the reason for all of that shit between me and her. He shouldn't have had her in my house, and she shouldn't have wanted to be there. I've been gone for a little over ten months, and this nigga texted me just about every day, asking me where I am and to remind me that the cops were looking for me.

Me: *Fuck you and your girl! Leave me the fuck alone.*

Case: *Bet that!*

I put my phone on the nightstand and went to take my shower so that I could get ready for bed. An hour later, I was in bed and sleep found me easily.

The next morning, Mena woke me up to tell me that she would be home and that Oshea could stay with her. I was so damn happy about that because I didn't have to make any stops. By the time I got to WC General Hospital, I had twenty minutes to spare. Walking into the hospital, I was nervous but so excited. I walked up to the receptionist's desk.

"Hi, I'm looking for Ann Price. I'm Honesty Gaines. I'm supposed to start work today." I smiled at the lady.

"Hey, Honesty. I'm Ann, come around and have a seat. I'll be training you today. The job is fairly easy, but it can get busy some days. We have to be on point today. I heard the new owner is going to be coming in this week, but no one knows exactly when. Just keep your head down, do your job, and you'll be fine."

* * *

Two Weeks Later

I was in such a good space and loving every minute of my job, and to top it all off, today was payday. I couldn't wait to get off and go to the Galleria to buy my baby some clothes. Everyone here seemed so nice and professional, and Ms. Ann was the coolest manager ever. But her ass was nosey and knew all the business around here. If you wanted to know what doctor or nurse was fucking who, all you had to do was ask Ms. Ann. Her and Ms. Rose kept me laughing. Ms. Rose was such a cutie pie. She was older but could dress her ass off and was always flirting with the men.

"He's here today, so y'all be on your best behavior," Ms. Ann stated, taking a seat behind the desk.

"Who's here?" Ms. Rose questioned, looking over the brim of her glasses.

"The new owner. I just saw them back in the emergency room department, and good God from Zion, that man is fine, young looking, and black," she said, fanning herself. I burst out laughing because these old ladies were a mess.

"Well, that's not the owner, because I heard somebody from the Crest family was taking over, and we both know the Crest family was white. The man I seen was black, but he did have some beautiful eyes. Mmmmm, mmmmm, it should be a crime to look that damn fine. Just wait, y'all gone see what I'm talking about.

Honesty, our asses are too old, but baby, you need to come to work like you're posing for the cover of People and catch you a rich nig...I mean, a rich man. Sorry, I almost forgot where the hell I was at." She laughed, and I was in tears.

"I'm good, I just made things official with my boyfriend last night." I smiled. Rob and I were in such a good place, and for the last week, I've been spending a lot of my time with him at his place. Even when he's not home, me and Oshea are there. He even said if I wanted to stay there with him, I could. I'm not sure if I'm ready to do all of that yet. The time I've been spending over there is enough for me right now.

"Ladies, I'm going to the cafeteria to get something to a muffin until lunch. Y'all want something?" I asked as I stood to leave.

"No, I'm good, baby," Ms. Rose stated, and Ms. Ann just shook her head no because she was helping a patient. When I made it down to the cafeteria, it was crowded in here, and I was just trying to get my blueberry muffin and leave.

"Honesty! Come here." Dana waved me over, and I hurried over to her. "Girl, what is going in here this morning? Chile, these new owners got everyone in a frenzy. They were just in here, so everybody's been trying to get next to him and kiss ass, I guess. You should hear these nurses coming in here gushing all over him. He fine now, I'm not gone hold you, but they doing too damn much." She shook her head, and I laughed.

"Dang, he must be fine. Because Ms. Ann said she's seen him, and her ass said the same thing," I told her.

"Yep. What you doing this weekend? You should come with me to this party at club Luxe on Saturday." She smiled, while ringing up my things.

"I'll have to let you know. I don't really have anyone to watch my son unless my cousin can do it, and normally, she be out in these streets." I laughed. Because Mena don't be playing. She doesn't have any responsibilities. It's just her, and my cousin is young, got a good job, and she's absolutely beautiful. So, I don't blame her for living her best life out here.

"Just let me know later," she stated and continued to help the people in line. I grabbed my things and headed back out front to the main receptionist's desk. This hospital was so freaking beautiful and had all kinds of stuff inside. I heard the doctors have rooms that they can check into like a hotel room to sleep if they're doing a double. The same with the nursing staff, and that shit was dope. Being here in this professional surrounding made me want to go to nursing school. The past couple of days I've definitely been looking into it. When I made it back up front, there were some cops, hospital security, and a detective talking to Ms. Ann, and Mrs. Jones from HR was also talking with them, and they were looking at me.

"That's her right there." Mrs. Jones pointed at me, and Ms. Ann looked at her with a frown on her face.

"Honesty Gaines, you're under arrest for the assault of Ms. Shanaisha Jackson. We've been looking for you for quite a while, and it wasn't until you got that speeding ticket and a background check was pulled by this hospital," she said to me with a smirk on her face.

"What! Nooo, I didn't do anything to anyone! I have a son! You can't take me to jail!" I cried, and the minute the cops grabbed me, I lost my mind and started swinging on them. I couldn't go to jail, my child needed me. They threw me to the ground and handcuffed me. Not only was I embarrassed and in pain from the impact, I was pissed. Everyone was looking at me, and all I could think about was my job. It was bad enough I started working before my six weeks was up, due to me needing to provide for my son. Now there was a possibility that I was going to lose my job.

"Stop! You don't have to do that shit to her!" Ms. Ann yelled, clearly getting upset at how they were treating me. I was hysterical and scared as shit right now. People were staring at me and recording the whole thing. What the fuck was going on! The moment they lifted me off the floor, was the moment our eyes met, and I was in total shock as Trust, his brother, and a group of men were standing there watching the altercation as they drug me out of the hospital with Ms. Jones screaming that I was fired. I never thought I would see him again, and definitely not like this.

Chapter Nine

TRUST

$\mathcal{W}$e've been touring the hospital that I just took ownership of for the last week. I was standing here in the lobby with my lawyers, the hospital executives, and my brother when we heard and saw this big commotion in the main entrance of the hospital. I was emotionally drained and overwhelmed, but I knew I had to get these tours done. I was hoping today would go by smoothly because tomorrow I had to tour a few more staples in the city but hearing this loud ass lady made my fucking head hurt. They have this woman screaming and crying. Even in her distressed moment, I'll never forget that voice.

"What's going on?" I asked, looking over at the lady that was just screaming she was fired.

"She assaulted someone months back in Philadelphia, and they're just getting her." She shrugged, smiling in my face like her ass was happy it happened.

"That child didn't deserve that. She's a nice girl and worked hard here, so she could take care of that beautiful baby of hers. Janice, you're wrong for firing her without letting the courts decide if she's guilty or not. Y'all could have taken this off the floor and in private and let them do what they needed that way. But we know you're messy like that," one of the receptionists stated.

"You said she has a baby?" I asked out of curiosity because I couldn't believe she had a baby by that nigga Case.

"Yes, and that child needs to be with his mother." She looked at me, and I quickly moved to the exit with my team walking with me. By the time we made it out front, they had already left.

I turned to my attorney, Jason. "Can you get me everything on her and this situation she's in? And Ms. Jones, is it?" I asked, looking at this bitch that wasted no time firing Honesty.

"Yes, sir." She smiled the biggest smile resting her hands on her wide hips. The sister was beautiful, and had a nice body, but that shit doesn't always move me.

"Since we're in the firing mood today, you're fired!" I looked at her with a smile.

"Yes sir! Use that executive thug ass power, baby bro. Whewwww, it's a new sheriff in town!" Taj animated ass said, looking around at these damn people.

"Fired for what! I've been at this hospital for fifteen years, and I run the show here in human resources!" She spat.

"And you've been treating the staff bad for years. The only reason you've been around so damn long is because you kept your legs opened to the CEO. Chile, don't get me started on the foolery that goes on around here," the receptionist that was taking up for Honesty stated.

"Ohhh shit! It seems that WC General got more drama than the hood. I gotta bring madear over here tomorrow, so she can get caught up." Taj laughed. I knew that I could fire her because since I've taken ownership, I wanted to learn more, and I was a quick learner. So I had my lawyers give me a quick crash course on legal things I needed to know about operating a business like this. I damn sure don't know everything, but what I do know is I can fire her ass.

"Pennsylvania is an at-will state, and I can fire you whenever I see fit without reason. But I'll give you this. Start treating people with grace. You never know what they may be going through. Yes, she was arrested, but she hasn't been convicted or tried for anything. The Thanksgiving and Christmas holidays are vastly approaching, and no one wants to be in this situation right now. Security, escort to remove her things and get her out of the building."

"Yesss, I love a man that takes charge. Welcome to Winter Crest General Hospital, sir. My name is Ann Price; I'm the receptionist manager here. Do what you can for that young lady because she's having a tough time right now," she said to me.

"I actually know Honesty, and we will do what we can to help her." I smiled, and we walked off to see when I could to talk to Honesty. Everything has been moving so damn fast since we've been here.

A couple of days after we arrived, I came over to the hospital, they did a DNA test on me and matched it with my deceased father. He was indeed 99.9 percent my Pop. Madear and Taj been wearing my ass out every time I say the word nigga or if I say something that doesn't sound like something black people would say.

The moment paternity was determined, they took me into Sanders and Associates law firm, and I spent days with these attorneys. My mind was blown at all the things that I own, and this thriving beautiful city was one of them. Not to mention, the hotel that we stayed in when we first got here, and my pop had just signed a deal to buy the hospital a day before he died. One damn day! This dude was filthy fuckin' rich, and when you speak about generational wealth, this was it. My children, great grandchildren, and their children are already rich, and they're not even born yet.

"Mr. Williams, I have someone from Sanders going down to represent her and she's waiting on you to meet her there if you want to speak to the young lady."

"Thank you, I'll be in touch." I shook their hands, and Taj and I left the hospital.

"What are the odds of us seeing, Hostage here? That's some crazy shit!" Taj stated as we headed downtown. It took my driver about twenty minutes to get through the downtown traffic, but when he pulled in front of the precinct, I got out and went inside.

"Mr. Williams, I'm Amanda Abraham, the attorney sent over from Sanders and Associates. Right this way, sir. They have a room for us to speak with Ms. Gaines in," she stated, and I followed behind her. Ten minutes later, Honesty was led into the room, and her tear-stained face and disheveled clothing pissed me the fuck off. She breathed a sigh of relief when she saw me sitting here, and I felt compelled to help her.

"Ms. Gaines, I'm Attorney Abraham. Mr. Williams has hired me to represent you. I've gone through the charges and read the report that Ms. Jackson filed against you. Do you know the fight she's referring to?" She asked Honesty, and I looked over at her.

"Yeah, it was almost a year ago, so I'm confused as to why they're bothering me now. I was away for a little over a week, and when I got home, my boyfriend at the time, had another woman in my house. Emotions were high, and we all got into a fight," she cried, wiping the tears from her face. All of this shit happened when she left my house. That nigga Case is a pussy. He did this shit to the girl, and then he allowed his new bitch to press charges.

"There is also a claim that she was pregnant and lost the baby. I'm still waiting on more information on that, because the dates from the hospital in Philadelphia haven't been sent over. If that comes back to be true, and she lost her child because of the fight with you, then we have a bigger problem," she said to her.

"Oh, my God. I can't go to jail or stay here. Who's going to take care of my so..." She paused and looked over at me.

"I just have to get out of here." She sat back in her chair and wiped her tears.

"Amanda, can I speak to her for a minute?" She stood from the chair and walked out.

"Didn't think I'd ever see you again, Swiper. I know this shit is fucked up and because your nigga is a bitch and I know you don't deserve this, I'm going to help you. Is there anyone you need me to reach out to or call?" I asked her.

"Thank you. No, they let me use the phone, and I called my cousin already. Please help me get out of here. I can't stay in here overnight, please help me. This all happened the night you let me go, and I beat both of their asses. I was fed up with him, and I just blew up on them. Case has put me through so much, and that was it for me. So, I moved out here with my cousin," she cried.

"I'll do what I can to help you. Just don't say shit to anyone, but Amanda. Just know that I'm here, and we gone work this shit out. I should tell they ass how you got me for 200 hundred racks, though." I laughed and so did she.

"I'm sorry, but you know your non-kidnapping ass shouldn't have taken me." The smile on her face was what I wanted to see.

"You right, my thug ass should've stuck to the shit I knew. But look, I have to go. Just know that my team is working on getting you out." I stood and when I pulled her in for a hug and the day I slid inside of her flashed through my mind, and my dick got hard. Amanda came back into the room and promised that she would call me as soon as she went in front of the judge. I told her that I would pay the bail once we knew what it was. I had an important meeting to attend in the next hour.

I still can't believe all that's happened to me and my family. I had some decisions to make about my drug operation because things had definitely changed. The news is out that Winter Crest is being taken over by the sole heir of Armon Crest III and his illegitimate kid is a black man. Now that's some news for your ass, and these people's heads are spinning.

Chapter Ten

HONESTY

*T*his shit was crazy, and I was scared out of my mind. I couldn't believe that Case and his bitch filed charges against me. Thank God I wasn't being charged for her losing a baby. My lawyer said the pregnancy couldn't be proven, so that was thrown out. It took ten hours for me to see a judge and to have my bail posted. My life flashed before my eyes, and I lost my mind when those cops grabbed me. All I kept thinking about was my son, and what would happen to him if I couldn't get myself out of this situation.

Seeing Trust in the hospital shook me to the core for many reasons. I was embarrassed that he had to see me like that, and how do I explain having Oshea to him? Even though I had a whole new pot of problems brewing due to his arrival, I appreciated him helping me get out of jail. I would figure out everything else as it came like I always did. My freedom was the most important thing, and I had that.

Case had some fucking nerve. Not only did the nigga have me kidnapped and took his time getting me back, he had the nerve to have a bitch and child laid up in my shit. I bowed out and let him and the bitch have each other, and he had the nerve to have me locked up? And right at the fucking holidays? He better not let me see his bitch ass nowhere.

"Hon, does he know that you have his son?" Mena questioned, and my tears immediately started falling, because I knew what I was up against. No matter the outcome, there was no way I should have held onto something so important.

"Babe, you gotta tell him. He deserves to know that he has a child, and if he rejects his son, then that shit would be on him, but you neglecting to tell him is wrong on so many levels," she stated, and I was ready to get my son and go hide out until I could figure out how to break this to him. Mena said that she met up with Ms. Ann to get my belongings, and she got her friend to take her to pick up my car. I was so damn grateful.

"I'm going to talk to him. I still can't believe that he's here and is the owner of Winter Crest." I sighed.

"What! Who's the owner of Winter Crest?"

"Trust is the owner. My lawyer said that it was good for me that he was on my side. She said he even spoke with the DA about my case. I'm praying this gets dropped, but for now, I have to go through all of this until it's resolved," I told her.

"OMG! I have been hearing about this shit all over the news. They said this dude was only twenty-eight years old, and his fucking net worth was crazy sick, like over ten billion dollars. Are you positive that Oshea is his child 'cause babbbby, that baby rich-rich! And if I was your ass, I'd be on his doorstep right fucking now with my clothes and my damn grey blue-eyed, Hawaiian skinded, chocolaty tented baby." She laughed with her crazy ass.

The complexion of Trust and this baby was something crazy, but beautiful as hell. I looked at my son every day in disbelief. I was still shocked that he came out of me. Only my fucked-up luck ass would push out my kidnapper's baby. The money sounded good, but I knew that more money brought more problems. Long as he did right by his son, I was good. That is if his ass didn't kill me first. How do you even tell a man you have a fucking secret baby by him? Especially a man like Trust. This shit was all bad.

Ten minutes later, we were pulling up to the house, and a Suburban was parked in the driveway.

"Who the fuck is that?" Mena asked, pulling up beside the truck.

"I don't know." I shrugged as we got out of the car. I was ready to get the stench of the jail off me. Once I showered and ate, I was going to cuddle with my baby since he was fast asleep and reach out to Ms. Ann to see if I could come back. I knew I was fired, but it was worth a shot. Billionaire baby daddy or not, oatmeal was better than no meal, so I was taking my ass to work to make my fucking oats. I may have lost the hospital job, but Winter Crest was a big city. I prayed I could find something else, especially before Christmas. My son was too young to know what the holiday meant, but I did want to get Mena some nice gifts. She'd been a Godsend to me and my baby. From holding my leg during labor and delivery to opening her doors to us. I owe her everything.

Ignoring the Suburban, I grabbed my baby's carrier out of the back-seat, and when I closed the car door, I got the shock of my life. It was him, and my heart dropped instantly.

What the fuck was he doing here and why? I wanted to hall ass in the house with my baby and slam the door. I knew I had to face Trust, but I wasn't ready. If I had it my way, I would wait till after the holidays, maybe a little after the first of the year, so I could build up confidence. I was scared shitless, and I don't scare easy, but my heart was definitely in my ass. I wasn't expecting things to happen so fast. Shit, I'm just seeing him for the first time today. I don't think I have the strength to tell him everything now.

"Uhhhh, Mena, can you take him inside?" I tried to get her to take him in so Trust wouldn't see him until I could talk to him about Oshea.

"Mmmm, mmmm. My hands are full." This heifer didn't have shit in her hand but a damn soda and a pack of Skittles. I wanted to drop kick the shit out of her ass. She was on her playful shit and wasn't shit about this situation comical. If she could get past Trust's looks and knew how this man was really coming, she wouldn't be protesting. It was not only in my best interest that this nigga didn't get mad but hers too. He was liable to kill me and her just off GP.

I shifted the carrier from my right to my left hand and turned my attention to Trust. I almost melted because this man was so freaking beautiful. Gosh, my son was a newborn version of him.

"He...Hey. What are you doing here? How did you even know where I lived?" I questioned, trying to pull the blanket over my baby's face. Thank God it was dark outside, so he couldn't quite get a good view of him.

"I hired your attorney, baby girl. She called and told me that you were released. She gave me your address, and phone number, and here I am. Is it alright if we go inside? I don't think the baby needs to be outside in the cold." Hearing him say that had me stuck. My damn feet felt like cement was holding them down.

"Sure." Is all I said, and headed inside.

Winter Crest weather seemed to be different from the rest of Pennsylvania. It was not far from the Poconos, so It got cold cold here. Snow started in October. We didn't have to wait till the winter months for it to look like the damn north pole.

"Have a seat," I told him.

Mena had pulled her decorations from the attic, so her eight-foot flock tree that was bulging out of the box, along with about ten large bags of tree décor from Hobby lobby sat in the corner of the living room. My cousin didn't play about her home. She kept it clean, smelling good, and the interior was immaculate. Her home was so cozy. I loved everything about it. Judging but the nod of approval, Trust was loving it too.

"I appreciate that. From my conversations with the DA and Amanda, I'm sure this will go away. I have Saud going to pay Case a visit because that was a bitch move. We don't do rats. Even if he wasn't the one to file the charges, he put the battery in that hoe's back. That was good as snitching."

I licked my chapped lips and looked down at the carrier to make sure my baby was covered.

"So, is this your place?" He asked.

"No, it's my cousin's place; she let me come stay with her. Now that I have a baby the space is kind of tight here. I'm not doing well finan-cially, so we're here until I can afford to move out. My boyfriend wants me to move in with him, but I'm not ready for that yet. I was so happy about my job at the hospital, because that was a step in the right direction for me. But as you know, I got fired, and now I'm back to square one. Hopefully, I can find something else soon." I smiled.

Telling my broke ass predicament was a pride killer, but at this point, I didn't give a damn. This man has seen me walk ass naked around his mansion—no reason for me to hold back from him now.

"I fired that chick. She reacted without getting all of the facts, and that shit wasn't cool. You still have your job. Take a couple a couple of weeks to get yourself together. I'll make sure your salary is paid..." He was interrupted by what he was saying because the baby started screaming at the top of his lungs, and my ass got nervous.

"Damn, you really had a baby. That's a blessing, though. Time know it be flying. It seems like it was just yesterday that your annoying ass was singing in my intercom? How old is he?" He asked. Trust rested his elbows on his knees and stared a hole through me. Here was this rich ass man was, dressed in his Sunday's best, dapper than a bitch. This man went from street nigga to rich tycoon, and he wore both hats very well. All that fine shit didn't mean nun though, because this man was straight action. If I picked my baby up and he had a glimpse of his eyes, it was over with.

"He's... ummm... two months."

"Oh ok. Let me see the young King." *This was it*. I damn near flatlined.

I just knew I was about to have a fuckin meltdown, and out of nowhere *Baby by Me by 50 Cent feat, Neyo* started playing. Mena had connected her phone to the soundbar and was milking this shit. This bitch was messy as fuck, and this nigga had the nerve to be nodding to the damn song waiting to see Oshea. I knew she was in her room laughing her ass off. It was no backing out now. I picked my baby up, because he was still crying. The moment I uncovered him and lifted him from his seat was the moment I could see the wheels in his head turning. Oshea was screaming his ass off, but there wasn't a tear in sight though, so that let me know this damn baby was just as messy as Mena.

Truth dropped his head and rubbed the back of his neck. He barely had a glimpse of the baby and had already established paternity.

"Honesty, I'm not going to play these games with you. Nor will I ignore the fact that this bab...that this baby favors me. He fuckin' favors me! What the fuck!" He yelled, I jumped, and the baby started screaming.

"You better open your fucking mouth and say something. Is he my son?" The anger in him was evident, and all I could do is look away and try to calm my baby. I could feel him burning a hole through me, and I knew I had to answer him, but I was so scared. I turned to face him, and the moment I saw his watery eyes caused my emotional ass to cry.

"Trust, I'm so sorry. I thought that I was pregnant by Case. You and I were only together one time, and it didn't cross my mind that he could be yours. I didn't realize he was yours until I actually gave birth to him. I didn't know how you would take the information; I was afraid of your rejection. I would never keep him from you. I was just trying to work through it all, but I was going to tell you."

Tears fell down my cheeks that were still cold from the weather. I was never the woman to do some shit like this. I wouldn't purposely keep a child from his father, but this shit just happened. Up until I gave birth over a month ago, I thought this was Case baby. I didn't have the chance to process my next steps. Plus, Trust is my damn kidnapper, and we live hours away from one another. For all I knew, Trust could have been dead or in jail!

"Do you hear yourself? When exactly were you planning to tell me? When he graduated from high school? The moment you pushed him out and realized you gave birth to my fuckin' twin should've been the same moment you reached out! Even if you had to drive your ass back to my fuckin' crib and sang in the got damn intercom system from the gate; *I got your baby!* You should have made that shit happen. So, yo' ass is just a fuckin' professional swiper, but you did your big one this time and swiped my muthafuckin' sperm and ultimately, my son! The fuck!" He yelled, becoming unhinged.

My son was crying so hard now that he was shaking. Baby Daddy or fucking not, he had me fucked up. He wasn't about to handle me like this, especially in front of my son. I didn't give a damn if he owned the whole damn United States!

"Get out! You're not going to talk to me like that! I don't give a fuck about your status in this town. Get the fuck out! We will talk about this when you can calm down and talk to me respectable!"

I was pissed off. I mean, I know this is on me, but we're not doing this shit tonight. I'm too stressed out right now, and I need to just calm down and regroup. He ignored me, took the baby from my arms, and held him close to his chest. He whispered something to the baby, kissed the top of his head, handed him back, and walked out. I walked over to the baby's bassinet, laid him down, and just let it go. I cried like a baby. I never wanted this to happen. I knew the longer I waited, the worse it would be.

"Geeesh! He mad, but guess what? His ass gone be alright. He needed to find out, because you would've kept putting it off. Oshea needs his dad, and I'm sure he will at least help you with your child financially. I just want the best for you, cousin. Now get you some rest because you've had a long day. 'Cause tomorrow night we're going to club Luxe to celebrate your newfound rich baby daddy," Mena stated, coming from the back. I wanted to ask her where she was when the nigga was going off on me, but I just told her I was down, as long as we could get Ms. Diane to babysit for me. Those Pink Pussies at club Luxe were the talk of the town, and I needed about six of them.

"I need a little peace, so I think I'ma go stay with Rob tonight. He didn't know that I got arrested until I called him when I got out of jail." I was a little disappointed that he didn't come over. Grabbing my phone from my purse, I sent him a text.

Me: *Do you mind if I come over?*

My Bae: *I'm not home right now, beautiful. I can meet you there in an hour; I'm a little tied up.*

Me: *Ok, call me when you're on your way home. I'm a little stressed, and I just want to be comfortable for a day or two. You know what? Don't worry about it, I can get me a hotel room. I forgot I got paid today before all the drama happened.*

My Bae: *Hell no. You can bring your fine ass to your man.*

Me: *K*

My mind went back to Trust and how angry he was with me, and my heart ached a little. I could see the pain in his eyes, and I truly never meant for that to happen. I packed a bag for me and Oshea and told Mena that I would see her tomorrow. I was drained from today's events and just needed a warm shower, a glass of wine, and Rob's comfortable bed. I pray tomorrow is a better day for me.

Chapter Eleven

TAJ

"This is some crazy shit! So, let me get this straight, she wasn't going to tell you at all about the kid?" I asked Trust as we all sat in the living room of his penthouse suite at the Elixar Resort.

"I don't know what the fuck she was going to do, man. I would've never found out about that kid had I not gone over there to check on her regarding her getting arrested. She said she was planning on reaching out to me, but I'm not sure when that shit would've been," I told him.

"Son, are you sure that he's yours? How did you meet this girl?" My mom asked, and I forgot she had no clue about my little kidnapping episode.

"Ma, that kid looks like me; it's absolutely no denying him. You would've thought you gave birth to your child all over again. I met her almost a year ago. I did something I shouldn't have done. Her dude gambled my money away and didn't pay me. And to be honest, I don't think he would've paid me. So, I went to his crib and took his girl until he bought my money." I shrugged.

"He had a hostage situation going on over there. Ion think he needs to be a kidnapper 'cause he doesn't do good with hostage negotiations. All them Christmas decorations he had up last year for Christmas was the hostage, not him. Chile, she took him for his money. That baby wore his ass out, you hear me. It was just a different type of kidnapper/hostage situation over there because you not supposed to sleep with or give your hostages babies. That's an express ticket to ten years, and that's your ass! And I mean that literally!" Madear was speaking so damn fast, her ass almost choked.

"I know holding that secret all this time almost took you out." Taj laughed.

"Damn sure did. I even thought about giving his money back a few times. But then I hit the blunt, and all of my senses came flowing back like the river of Jordan," Madear said, and I swear she had my ass on the floor.

"Trust, you can't be doing no shit like that. Your grandma is joking around, but she's right; things could've gone bad. Do you love her or is this something that just happened?" Ma asked him.

"It was something that just happened. The fact remains is that shorty knew where I lived." Trust was obviously upset, and I didn't blame him because all jokes aside, I would be ready to strangle her ass and raise my kid on my own. He was lying, though. He was in love because he always bring Hostage up, and if that ain't love ion know what is. He only fucked one damn time on a fucking whim and was sprung.

This shit was like a damn soap opera. I'm leaving in a few days to head back to Philly, and I was glad about it. I'm still knee deep in the drug game, but Trust wants us to come completely out, so that's what we're trying to do. He was going to turn the operation over to Saud but is now thinking about retiring him as well.

When my brother says that he got us for life, that's what he meant. I appreciate everything he's done and will continue to do for us. I'm a rich nigga already, and if he never gives me a dime of his money from his Pops, I'm still set for life, but old habits die hard. 'Cause when I found out his ass owned a damn city and hospital, the first thing I thought of is us being able to move all kinds of dope through this muthafucka. You know how much money we could make off a whole damn city? Plus, since my brother owned it, the laws couldn't do shit but allow it. I had to really think about it, because we didn't need to do that shit anymore. My brother's mindset is so differ-ent, and I knew once everything was laid out in front of him, he would formulate his own plan and hit the ground running. And that's exactly what he did.

It was a wonderful thing to see, and I'm excited just to have a front row seat and watch this dude elevate. I'm genuinely happy for him. He deserves everything that's happening in his life right now. His one request from his family is that we make the transition to live here in Winter Crest with him. My mom and Grandmother were born and raised in Philadelphia, so it's definitely a hard transition for them. They're leaving everything they know and are used to. I'm alright with being here with him. I don't have anything holding me back in Phil-adelphia. I'm going to always be wherever my family is.

"Bro, I don't have all the answers and I've never been in this type of situation before. But I know that things will work out. If that's your son, you still have those moments of watching him grow and not missing any of his special moments. I agree that the moment she had doubt, she should've figured out how to reach out to you. But we're past that now. You don't want to be in a bad space with her. Get the baby tested, and if he's definitely yours, then make your next move your best one. You know I'ma always be ten toes down for whatever you on," I told him.

"I know, man. I'll be alright, this shit just got me pissed. I love you guys and appreciate y'all for being here for me. I'ma call it a night. I have a lot on my mind, and I need to be ready for my meeting with the lawyers when we go do the tour of the Crest family estate," he said to us. We all agreed to call it a night, because we did have to get up early in the morning.

The next morning came faster than I wanted. My ass was tired as fuck.

"So, what do y'all think? I'm sure if I get things updated in here and make some additions, it could definitely add to its beauty." Trust looked over at us, and I agreed with him. If he had some folk to come up in here and change some shit up, it could work out. The mansion was immaculate on the outside but needed to be gutted like a rat on the inside. Shit looked like a whole damn African Safari in this bitch, and all the fucking wood over the walls was like a damn wild forest.

"Chile, yes because all these damn dead animals on the walls just ain't it!" Madear shook her head with her damn face all twisted. This is the reason we can't take her ass nowhere. She says what she wants. I think that's where I get the shit from, and I'm gone laugh at her ass every time.

"The men of the Crest family loved seasonal hunting, so that's why you see all of the animals adorning the walls," one of the Lawyers explained.

"Yeah, this new generation of Crest is from the hood. The only thing we're hunting is a bitch ass nig...Nevermind."

I had to remember who I was talking to. Every now and then, my gangsta shows up, and ion know how to stop that shit. I'm trying to change my ways, but that shit is hard! If you ask me, my brother might be the fucking descendant of the Klan, and this estate was the fucking proof. I could have sworn I saw a picture of a lynching in the main corridors. He'd better hope the Crest ghost didn't get his ass in his sleep. Fuck it, when he moved in, I was gone continue staying at the Elixar until I found my spot. I wasn't Crest blood, and ion need them Klan ghosts snatching my soul. Fuck all that.

"I think you can turn this place into yours in no time, son. I say keep it in the family, but just make it yours. Give it the vision you have for it." My mom patted his back trying to reassure him that his decision to keep the place was the right one and she was right. Since Thanksgiving was tomorrow, Trust wanted to add to the things that were already happening in the city for the holiday season. So today, he was giving out 40 tons of food for any family that wanted or needed it for their Thanksgiving dinner, no matter their financial status. This city was all about the holidays because the downtown area was lit up with fall harvest décor and shit. I done passed so many inflatable turkeys in yards that I didn't even want Turkey on my plate tomorrow. Hell, some folk even had on their Christmas lights and shit up.

We were all going down with him to participate in the festivities, and this weekend we would be there to see the lighting of the city Christmas tree down at City Hall. All of this is new for us, but from what we were told, these are traditions that his family was into. He wanted to keep that going because our mom was big on giving back during the holidays in Philly. A few hours later, we were passing out food and greeting some of the residents of Winter Crest. It felt good to see everyone happy about getting the help they needed. I even heard about a party Blaque Friday that was happening this weekend at Club Luxe. They said the club is a whole vibe, and that's exactly what we needed. Once we finished up, we were now heading back to the hotel to get some rest. I'd already had a stylist go to the galleria for our all-black attire. Trust didn't even know, but the business side was going to be put on pause so we could see what this WC pussy be like.

"Are you down to check out that party this weekend the girl was telling us about?" I asked Trust as we walked into the lobby of the hotel.

"Yeah, that sounds like the move. I need to unwind a little. But you know we have to be on some chill shit when we're in public. I'm sure these folks would love to see me fail. That's not the perception I'm trying to build here," he said to me.

"If it's some bullshit, then we can just get the fuck up outta there. Oh, and I got a call from Saud about that nigga Case. He said he was on some fuck y'all niggas type time. I'ma pay a visit to that nigga myself when I get back in Philadelphia."

"Nah, let him rock out. I'll pay that visit myself in due time," he said to me. I went upstairs to order some dinner and called it a night.

We didn't do much for Thanksgiving. Mom had dinner catered for us, and we enjoyed the time together relaxing and eating some good food. The next morning, we sent Madear and mom to do some Black Friday shopping while we smoked and talked more about the city. Now we were dressed and on our way to the club. Trust was still in his feelings about ole girl not responding to him.

"She still hasn't called you back?" I asked as the driver pulled in front of the club.

"Nah, but it's all good. I'm letting her have this one for the time being. I've been in a really bad place with this shit, and the next time I see her, I want to make sure I'm calm enough to have a decent conversation. She's definitely gone have to see me, so she might as well get ready for it." I knew at that point he was gonna show his ass.

Trust had security with us because there was no way that we could come without. People knew who he was, and hanging out without protection wasn't a good idea. This nigga was worth too damn much. Fuck around his ass will be the damn hostage! They had three different levels to the club, and I swear I was trying to go see what these skrippers was talkin' 'bout. But my brother wanted to go to the club part, so we were headed up to the VIP section they had for us.

Everyone was in their all black, and the bitches were bad as fuck. Winter Crest had women that looked like they came from another planet, and I was ready to sample. This club was lit as fuck, and I could tell a lot of money had been poured into it. *FNF By Glorilla* was blasting through the speakers, and this shit was a vibe for sure. The bottle girl that was assigned to us came to take our orders, and a few minutes later, she was back with different bottles placing them on the table.

"Isn't that Hostage over there?" I asked Trust. It looked like her, but I wasn't sure 'cause the last time I saw her ass, she looked like Taraji crazy ass did when she played in that movie Acrimony.

"Yeah, that's her." Is all he said. Getting up from his seat, he walked down to the section where Honesty was sitting with a few girls, and I followed behind him.

"So, is the reason you're ignoring my calls!" He angrily spat, and I thought the nigga gave this speech about being in the public eye and not acting up. It looks to me like his ass was about to act up.

"Me being here is my business, and I was planning to call you tomorrow when I had some free time to talk without interruption," she told him, and he just stood there in deep thought. And at this point, we should all be afraid of what those thoughts are.

"Damn, you fine as fuck!" Her friend yelled out, looking over at me. I licked my lips because I will fuck this girl senseless. I need me some local pussy, and baby girl can definitely get these fuckin' inches.

"Nah, we gone have that discussion now, and he grabbed her hand, but some dude ran up on him. And that was the wrong fucking move because security was on his ass quick.

"Nigga, get yo' fuckin' hands off of my girl! What the fuck is wrong with you?!" This nigga yelled and Trust burst into laughter.

I had to give it to the nigga. He was rocking Gucci and had a lil' chain and watch on in his all black. But that was lil nigga shit to us. Looks like Hostage done went and got her another Case. I was gone fasho' tell her she needed to know how to pick 'em. She seemed to be attracted to the damn yes men. At least she trapped the boss though, so she just might know a lil' sum.

"Rob, calm down. This is my son's father, and he just wanted to talk." She tried to calm her dude.

"Fuck that! He can talk to both of us about our kid. Where the fuck was he when he was born? I was there! That's my fuckin' son, nigga!" This nigga Rob yelled, and before we could react, Trust was on his ass. I had to get him off him quickly and get my brother out of the club.

"We have unfinished business! So, I'ma see you real soon!" He gritted. Security got us out of there before shit got bad.

"Nigga! What the fuck were you thinking? There are too many eyes in the club, and if that nigga knows who you are, he could be on some bullshit! We got to think before reacting, bro," I said to him as security sped out of the parking lot. I guess her nigga may be a problem, but when it comes to his kid, that nigga needs to step away and let them handle it. Because I would hate to see this shit get out of hand and fucking with Trust, it can definitely go left.

Chapter Twelve

TRUST

I was about to explode! I've been pacing back and forth in this fuckin' suite. Like, who the fuck this nigga talking to! It's the fact that he's rubbing that shit in, calling my child his! The fuck? And this bitch just standing there like shit was all good! Where was that nigga when she needed to get the fuck out of that jam, she was in a few days ago? But this nigga can talk about him being there when he was born? Plus, how the fuck was it that this nigga got to be around my son, but I didn't know he existed? That shit was foul! My baby probably was already familiar with this lame ass nigga. I was so pissed I was ready to say fuck this town and burn this bitch to the ground just because Honesty was walking it's grounds while taking me for a simp ass nigga.

Fuck that! I'm not going out like that at all. There are certain things I don't play about. That's my family and a nigga that feels like he can play in my fuckin' face! I pulled my phone out and sent her a text.

Me: *I need to see you right now!*

Honesty: *That shouldn't have happened, and I'm sorry he got involved. I'll be available tomorrow.*

Me: *That doesn't work for me. Pack you and the baby some things; I'm* *coming to pick you up. I have a room here in my suite that you can stay in, just for a couple of days. I need to see him, and we need to get a DNA test done right away.*

A blind man could see that baby was mine, so a DNA wasn't necessary, but I tossed that shit in there to let her know I meant business.

Honesty: *I'm with my boyfriend, and I'm staying at his house this weekend. I can meet you tomorrow to talk, and we can get the test done next week.*

Me: *I'm not playing this game with you. I've missed all of this time with him! And you got this nigga out here talking shit about what he's done? I want you in my suite with my son tonight. Either you're coming willingly or well... you know how this shit goes. You done been there, done that. Either way, I'll see you soon, baby girl.*

Honesty: *What! Like I said, I'll see you tomorrow.*

I stopped texting her and dialed Taj's number.

"Sup, bro?" He picked up on the first ring.

"I need to make a run, and I need for you to take this ride with me. I'm driving so no security on this run. I'll meet you in the lobby in twenty minutes, I need to change my clothes. Oh, strap up." I ended the call and went to change my clothes. By the time I made it down to the lobby, Taj was coming out of the gift shop with a pack of damn M&M's and a bottled water.

"What's up? You good?" He questioned with a concerned expression.

"I'm gucci. I asked shorty to come see me, so I need to go get her." I shrugged, turning to walk out the door, and my car was sitting out front. The parking attendant passed me my keys, we got in the car and pulled off.

"Nigga! Don't be on no bullshit. I mean, is she aware that we're coming to get her?" He asked, looking over at me.

"Yes, she's aware that I'm coming, and I told her I would see her soon."

Twenty minutes later, we were pulling into the driveway of Honesty's cousin's house. Her cousin's car was in the driveway, so I hope she was home. We got out the car and rang the doorbell.

"Who is it?" She asked.

"Trust." She opened the damn door so quick, as if she was expecting me.

"She's not here; she's at Rob's house." She smiled but had all of her attention on Taj.

"Do you have his address?" I asked her.

"Now you know I can't give you that, because if you hurt my cousin, we're going to have problems. I'm rooting for y'all because she's been though a lot and deserves happiness, but that's still my family. Right or wrong, I'm rocking with her," she said to me. I respected her for not folding on her family but fuck all that. I needed this nigga's address like yesterday.

"I'm not sure if I can give her that, but I would like to get to know my kid. I just need that address, and I promise you she won't be hurt in any way."

"Like I said, I can't give you that information. I just know there's this banging ass street over by the Cove Projects called Brickell Ave. The bodega on that block got these fire steak sandwiches. Normally the house next door to it will let you park in its driveway." She shrugged.

"What! Say your fine ass giving us the address without saying that shit!" Taj said to her. The shit was funny because my ass was trying to run all that shit through my mind and hoped I remembered what the hell she said.

"Oh, you want me to be direct? I'll see you when you're done handling business, daddy. I hope your girl don't mind sharing." She bit down on her bottom lip.

"Say less." He pulled her into him, gripping her ass, and his nasty ass stuck his tongue out, licking her lips. I had what I needed and turned to walk back to my car. A few minutes later, Taj came running out to the car.

"Lil mama fucking with the wrong damn one, but I'ma give her a quick muthafuckin' lesson tonight. I'ma dog walk the shit out of that pussy. Let's make this shit quick." He adjusted in his seat and sat back.

I sent Honesty another text, and she didn't even respond, so I put the Cove projects in my GPS. Just as long as I got to the area of where this nigga lived, I was good. She could've just given me the address, but

I guess this shit works. I don't know why she was testing my patience like she didn't know the type of nigga I am, but I damn sure didn't mind reminding her.

It took me about fifteen minutes to make it over to that side of the city, and it didn't take me long at all to find the street or the store that her cousin was talking about. I parked on the corner of the block.

"Let's go, bro." I got out of the car and called Jerry on FaceTime. He picked right up.

"Hey, boss. Do you have what I told you to get?" He asked.

"Yes, I got it," I told him, as I walked up to the door of this nigga Rob's house.

"Why the hell you call his ass? And why the fuck you putting that in these damn people locks?" Taj ass started looking around and shit.

"Just pull your gun out and get ready." I turned my attention back to the phone.

"Put that tool in the lock and turn it until you hear the lock click." I did everything Jerry told me to do, and minutes later, the lock clicked. Pulling my gun out, I turned the knob, and we were moving inside the house.

"Nigga, I thought you said she was waiting for us to pick her up. Yo' ass gotta stop taking these niggas girl, and if you gone keep taking the same damn girl, just keep her ass with you. I can see the headlines now. The new dumb ass Crest Heir throws away all of his billions to kidnap women for a living! Then she got a baby with her? This shit low key trafficking. I should have stayed with lil hot and ready. A wet pussy sounds a hell of alot better than a hot and a fuckin' cot!" Taj whispered.

Ignoring his ass, I moved upstairs, opening doors until I found the right one. I could hear snoring coming from the room. I lightly shoved the door open, and we eased into the room. It was definitely a nostalgic moment. She had the sleep mask over her eyes, while rain music playing from what I assumed was her phone since the tv was off, and all I could do was stare at her.

"Niggggaaa! Are you gone snatch her ass or wait for the police to show up, and we go to jail!" Taj gritted, trying to keep it down and not wake this nigga up. He was at the club, so maybe he was drunk and out like a light, but at this point, I really didn't give a fuck.

"Get the baby and the bag," I whispered to Taj. I turned back to lift Honesty in my arms, and she did exactly what I thought she would do, nestled into my chest, and kept sleeping. Taj grabbed the baby and his bag. I saw her purse on the nightstand next to her phone, so I grabbed both and crept out of the room. Baby girl slept hard as fuck, because she still didn't move. I don't know how the hell she cared for a baby at night. I just know his cries don't wake her. I saw a coat hanging by the door. I told Taj to grab and place it over her, and that's the moment she stirred in my arms and quickly removed the mask.

"What the fuck!" She spat, and we moved outside while she tried her best to fight me and get out of my arms.

"Put me the fuck down! What are you doing here? I'm not going anywhere with you! I told you I would see later today!" She yelled. I grabbed the keys from her purse and passed them to Taj so that he could get the baby buckled in.

"I can't believe you! So, you just gone kidnap me again? You do know this shit is against the law. You can't just keep breaking into people's shit and taking me out of their bed," she spat, mad as hell.

"You right! This nigga doesn't give a fuck. Your ass just a hostage again. Gone and get in the car, so y'all can work this shit out, 'cause he gone keep coming back," Taj told her as he shut the door. I placed her in the car, passed Taj the keys to my car, and I drove hers because the baby's car seat was already in the car.

"I'll see you later." I knew he was going back to ole girl's house, and I had to deal with my situation.

"This isn't how you're supposed to do this. You can't keep doing this shit to me just to get your way." She looked over at me as I backed out of her nigga's driveway.

"I told you I wanted to talk. I'm not into waiting when I want something." I looked over at her, and she was staring out of the window. I was glad her ass didn't argue back because I'm sick of the back and forth with her. I just wanted to come to common ground about our son that I still hadn't held yet. We finally made it back to the hotel, and I got out the car to get the duffle bag she said she had in the trunk. She slid on a pair of sweats, a t-shirt, and put some slides on her feet. A few minutes later, we were on the elevator heading up to my penthouse.

"Make yourself at home. Do you need anything?" I asked her.

Prior to getting her out of jail, it had been a while since I have seen her. I never thought that she would ever be back in this house. I missed her being here with me.

"No, I'm fine. Look, I know you're upset, and I'm sorry. He's your child; we both can see that, but where do we go from here because I don't want to fight with you? I fucked up, but I had to get my shit together. The baby isn't that old, as you can see, and you didn't live around the corner. He can barely stay awake more than three hours at a time and can't even hold his head up yet. He's still a newborn, so you haven't missed anything. The last time we had any type of interaction, you were rude and told me to leave.

I didn't think you would hear me out, especially me coming to tell you I had your baby. Rob helped me out a lot during my pregnancy, but he didn't have to do what he did at the club. I'm sorry about that. He was way out of line. If it makes you feel better, he doesn't have much interaction with the baby. He's always running the streets, and never really home. My cousin and I are all Oshea knows, and the babysitter that I get to keep him from time to time. Hearing her say that nigga name had me ready to fuck his ass up.

"That nigga disrespectful, and if that's my son, I don't want him near my kid. Is that my son?" I nodded down at the baby, never taking my eyes off her.

"Yes." She looked away, and I walked up on her, making her face me.

"I'm not trying to argue. I need to spend time with him, and I need for you to allow me that time. This all has happened so damn fast, and as I'm trying to grasp it all. I still need to be close. I know you're not going to leave your baby with us, so I'm inviting you to be here with me. I'm trying this approach because screaming and yelling isn't going to get us far. Are you living with your nigga or are you living with your cousin?" I asked her.

"Ok, I don't want to fight either. Let's work together and figure things out for the sake of our son. I wasn't trying to hide him; I just needed time. I live with my cousin, but I spend a great deal of time with Rob." She sat down on the couch, and I took the baby from his carrier and held him in amazement.

* * *

Two Weeks Later

hings have definitely changed between Honesty and I. The best part of it all is that the DNA came back that Oshea is my son. Honesty and I are in a better space as friends and doing what's needed to raise our child. We even took some time to get to know each other a little better. She's even staying a few days out of the week here with me so that I can bond with my him. She's having a hard time with her man, but that's not my problem, and I could care fucking less. I didn't like that nigga no fucking way. When she's here, I be hearing her screaming to the top of her lungs at his ass. Long as she doesn't disturb my son with that fucking hollering, we good. I hired the contractors and had them working overtime to get my house ready for before the Christmas holiday.

My mom and Madear settled on their house a few days ago. Madear felt like it was best that she stays with my mom, and mom was alright with that. They were both ecstatic about the baby, and my mom couldn't get enough of him. She loved on him every chance she got, and Taj was the same way with him. I'm so happy everyone was excited about having a new edition to the family. I was pissed when I found out about my son, but now, I could barely go to sleep without him being around. When he wasn't here, I was always on FaceTime with her just so that I could see him and talk to him. I was obsessed with him. If I knew this is what fatherhood felt like, I would have had a child a long time ago. I'd already met with my lawyers and started a trust for him, and added him as the beneficiary to my empire. My boy was set for life, and he didn't even know it. I was in my bedroom when Honesty walked into the room.

"Hey, I just wanted to thank you for putting the money in my account. Now I'm able to find a place for me and Oshea." She smiled.

"I told you you're welcome to stay with me. The house is huge, and it's just me. Oh, I forgot you got a nigga." I shook my head because she really liked that dude.

"Why do you do that? We're not together, and I'm sure you have plenty of women flocking at your feet. You're the talk of the town. All the women want the fine ass billionaire that owns the city. I already know I'm not what you're looking for. You haven't tried to come at me not once." She nervously chuckled, but something was off.

I saw a glimpse of sadness in her eyes. The only reason I haven't tried her is because of her being with her nigga. Pulling off my shirt so that I could jump in the shower, I walked up on her, and she stepped back a little.

"Don't ever assume anything about me. You have a nigga, and I'm trying to respect you because of your situation. And that's heavy on the you part. I don't give a fuck about that nigga. Shorty, anytime you feel like you want to jump on this dick, come crawl in that bed, and I'ma give you everything you're looking for." I smiled, kissing her forehead, and left her shaking ass standing right there to go take my shower.

Once I was done, I walked out of the room to go say goodnight to my baby boy.

"Hey, just want to kiss my boy goodnight," I said to her, walking into the room.

"Ok." She was deep into texting on her phone, so she never looked up at me. I kissed Oshea and walked out, heading back down to my bedroom. I crawled into bed and turned my lamp off. I heard my bedroom door open, and I knew it was her.

"Before you get into my bed. Make sure this is what you want to do because there is no going back, Honesty. I'm not going to play these games with you, or your nigga 'cause I'll blow his brains out and leave your ass to cry at his funeral. I've been nice in so many ways when it comes to you, but I'ma stone-cold killa, and I need you to know that." She stood there thinking for a while, and I was alright with that because I wanted her ass to be sure she knew what she was doing. The moment she crawled in my bed, I snatched her little ass up, placing her on her back and removing every piece of clothing she had on. I placed kisses up and down her body. A moan escaped her lips just as I slid my fingers across her clit.

"I've been wanting you since the day you left my house in Philly," I gritted, crashing my lips against hers and siding my dick up and down her clit. The urgency to be in her had taken over me, and I eased my dick inside of her. We both let out a sigh.

"Ahhhh, fuck!" She cried out as the tears slid down her face. I started thrusting in and out of her, causing her pussy to grip my dick. The feeling was so fuckin' crazy. I've never had pussy so good in my fucking life. She held on as I continued to deep stroke her insides. Then she closed her eyes trying to stop the tears.

"Open your eyes, baby girl. Let me look at you." My pace picked up, and my strokes became deeper and deeper.

"Ohhh my Goddddd!" she cried out, digging her nails into my back.

"Urghhhhhhhhhhh!" I growled, slamming inside of her as we both started cumming. For the rest of the night, I got reacquainted with this beautiful woman. All I know is she just fucked up because there was no going back to that nigga. This girl had been invading my thoughts for damn near a year, and I was happy to know that I'd filled her womb with my seed. I wasn't letting her ass go this time. I don't give a fuck if I have to get a panic room built and lock her ass in there. Honesty was mine, and now that we shared a son, this shit was for life.

* * *

few days had past, and Taj and I were back in Philly to handle some business. The shit I was about to do I've been waiting to do for the longest fucking time. We were sitting here in the dark, waiting for this nigga to come home. I was smoking a cigar with my gun in my lap.

"Nigga, who the fuck you think you are, Scarface? And why we gotta sit in the muthafuckin' dark? The dark makes my ass nervous. I need to see a muthafucka coming my way," Taj ass whispered. A few minutes later, we heard the front door open, and I waited for my guest to join me in his living room.

"We wish you a merry Christmas! We wish you a merry Christmassssssss and a happy new fuckin' yearrrr! Damn, I miss that bitch." He laughed, and I assumed his bitch ass was drunk. The moment the lights came on, this nigga tried to go for his gun. I sent a shot to his leg because I wasn't ready to make it lights out for him just yet.

"How the fuck you get in my shit?" Case asked, and I kneeled down to him so he could hear me and hear me good.

"I know you felt like you had the upper hand, bitch, because you know how I felt about your uncle. But you're not gone ever hurt her again, bitch! I'll kill every nigga I have to over her! Thanks for owing me that money, though. We wouldn't have our beautiful son. Oh yeah, she gave me a handsome baby boy." I smirked, and this nigga looked like all the blood drained from his body. Then I put a bullet between his eyes. Fuck that nigga!

Saud came in, and I dapped him up on my way out. He would make sure that shit was cleaned up, and we no longer had to worry about his bitch ass. I let the nigga live way too long, and now that I had officially made Honesty mine, it wasn't enough room on the planet for the both of us. I'll do whatever it takes to protect her.

Chapter Thirteen

HONESTY

One Week Later

I have been losing my damn mind, and I know my ass is wrong for not ending things with Rob. Trust has had my ass in the air every fucking night since I went to him a week ago. I couldn't resist him any longer; I wanted him. He has changed my life in so many ways, and I'm so grateful for it.

"Honesty, I still can't get over that fine man being your baby daddy. Hunny, I know that's right. He stops by here every day to check on you. If you don't marry that boy, so these nurses can get the hell away from him," Ms. Ann fussed. I've been back at Winter Crest General for a week now, and even though I don't have to work, I want to. I love this place, and it looked so beautiful in here.

Trust put me in charge of decorating the hospital, and the team I hired did the damn thing. I was so damn excited about the way it looked. His house was complete, and I hired the same team to do his compound as well. He said he wanted his son to have everything he didn't have growing up, and he wanted his home to feel and be in the spirit during the holidays. I'm so glad he was over his feelings about

Christmas. Tonight, was the Winter Crest festival, and this will be our first time experiencing it.

"Uhhh, you got company. Two o'clock." Ms. Rose nudged me, and when I looked up, it was Rob headed towards the desk.

"Can I talk to you for a minute?" He asked. I stood from the desk and decided to take this talk outside.

"Hey, I was going to call you later today." I smiled at him.

"I bet the fuck you were. Ever since you've been on this co-parenting shit with this nigga, you've been on some bullshit," he gritted.

"Look, I know this isn't the right time to tell you this, but I think we should end this. You don't like him, and he's my son's father, so that means we're going to be spending time together. And to be honest with you, I still have feelings for him. I'm sorry, Rob. I don't want to lead you on or lie to you," I told him.

"Bitch! Fuck you! I've been fucking other bitches since I met your dumb ass." He pushed past me, and I was a little taken aback by what he just said. I don't believe him. Maybe he's just upset because I broke it off with him. I feel like a weight has been lifted off me, and now I can love this man freely. I walked back into the hospital all smiles, and for the rest of the day, I enjoyed being at work and celebrating in the Christmas festivities they had going on today.

I got a call from Amanda, and she told me that the DA dropped the charges. It was because of my connection to Trust. Either way, I was happy as fuck about that shit. I was going home tonight and riding his dick something serious as my thanks for all that he does for me. I couldn't wait for Christmas. I have our family pajamas all picked out, and even my cousin Mena was coming over to stay the weekend with us. She was in heaven over Taj's ass, and I'm definitely rooting for them. Taj is just a hard one to crack, but she wants this with him.

A few hours later, we were at the Winter Crest Festival, and it was such a joy to be a part of this. Watching the families that signed up to get their Christmas gifts was everything. The entire scenery was something to see. All of the trees were lit, and the courtyard of city hall was definitely a winter wonderland.

* * *

Christmas Day

 $\mathcal{T}$ his time last year, I was all over the place. The life that I once knew changed, but this year my life has changed for the better.

"Everyone is downstairs waiting for us." He walked up to me, kissing my neck.

"Ok, I'm ready to go down." I turned in his arms, smiling.

"Ohhhh my God! It looks absolutely amazing in here! You did that, cousin! This shit is so freaking dope," Mena said as she walked into the room. I had some changes that I wanted to the decorations, so they came out last minute to make those changes for me. I walked into the kitchen to see if Ma Regina needed any help.

"Hey, do you need help with anything?" I asked, sitting down at the counter.

"No, baby. I got it. Honesty, I'm happy things are working out for you and Trust. I know how you guys met wasn't ideal, and had I known what was going on, that shit would have ended. But I'm glad I got my grandson out of the deal. From the moment I laid my eyes on him, I was in love. I knew without a shadow of a doubt that he was my grand-baby. Trust may seem hard on the outside, but he has a big heart. Take care of his heart, and I believe my son will love and take care of you." She smiled and gave me a hug. A couple of hours later, we had our dinner and now was sitting around the family room drinking and passing out gifts.

"Having you and my son here with me makes it all worth it." He pulled me in for a kiss, and I wouldn't change anything about this moment. Trust gave me a diamond necklace and bracelet, and my mouth was on the floor because no one has ever given me anything like this. I didn't know what to get a man that has everything, so I got him clothes and sneakers. He always said I had an eye for nice pair of sneakers, because you could definitely catch me in a nice pair of kicks. We ate good, drank good, and now it was time to relax.

"I'm taking this cutie pie home with me. Y'all know me and mama need him to look out for us," Mama Regina said, walking into the family room with Oshea in her hands.

"Go right ahead. We've been drinking, and that gives us a chance to sleep in for a change," I told her. Trust didn't like to part from his son. He was definitely having separation issues when it came to his son.

"Hold on mom, I'll walk you out." He stood from his seat and placed a kiss on my lips before leaving the room. The moment I heard the door alarm chime I knew he was back in the house, and it was showtime!

"Joyyyyy to the worlllllddd the lord isss commmme... Let Earth receive her King...Let every heart prepare Him room... And heaven and nature sing...In Heavennnnn and nature sannnngggg!" I was in a fit of laughter singing through the intercom. I really fell out laughing when Trust came back into the family room with a sledgehammer crashing it against the intercom system. I guess it's safe to say, he doesn't like my singing. We both were in a fit of laughter, and this moment was the best thing ever. For the rest of the night we enjoyed each other, and our free time.

He balanced everything he has going on so well. I still can't believe he owns a damn city, a hospital, and a host of other businesses in Winter Crest. He may have gone through a trying time as a kid, but God blessed him immensely, and I feel just as blessed.

* * *

Four Months Later

"*F*uckkkkkkkk! I'm about to cum!" I screamed, as he pounded my insides.

"Stop playing and ride this muthafucka!" He gritted.

"I'm about to pull that cum! Oh, God, I'm cumming" I screamed, bouncing up and down on his dick.

"Yeah, give me all that shit," he growled, slamming into me over and over again until we both were moaning and cumming. We were breathing so damn hard I felt like I needed an asthma pump.

"I want you to marry me, baby," he said to me, and I quickly snapped my neck in his direction.

"What? You want to marry me? Are you forreal?" I had to ask him again because what the fuck? Was he serious?

"Is this serious enough for you?" He smiled, holding the biggest fucking princess cut diamond I've ever seen in person. I've always seen rings that big on television or on these celebrity wives' fingers.

"OMG! Yessss, I'll marry you, baby! But I have one request, can we please wait until I have your baby?" I looked over at him, and his eyes were big as saucers.

"No fuckin' way! You're pregnant?" He asked to be clear.

"Yes." I laughed, rubbing my stomach.

He jumped up, lifting me from the bed, giving me the biggest kiss, and sliding my ring on my finger. I was happy. We were happy, and I can't wait to spend the rest of my life with this man. Who would have thought him snatching my ass up twice would lead to this? I love Trust with everything in me, and I'm so grateful that he chose me to love.

The End

Printed in Great Britain
by Amazon